SK8ER

SK8ER

Steven Barwin

James Lorimer & Company Ltd., Publishers
Toronto

© 2007 Steven Barwin

James Lorimer & Company Ltd. acknowledges the support of the Ontario Arts Council. We acknowledge the support of the Government of Canada through the Book Publishing Industry Development Program (BPIDP) for our publishing activities. We acknowledge the support of the Canada Council for the Arts for our publishing program. We acknowledge the support of the Government of Ontario through the Ontario Media Development Corporation's Ontario Book Initiative.

Cover illustration:
Steven Murray

The Canada Council | Le Conseil des Arts
for the Arts | du Canada

ONTARIO ARTS COUNCIL
CONSEIL DES ARTS DE L'ONTARIO

Library and Archives Canada Cataloguing in Publication
Barwin, Steven

Sk8er / Steven Barwin.

(Sports stories)
ISBN 978-1-55028-985-5 (bound)
ISBN 978-1-55028-983-1 (pbk.)

I. Title. II. Title: Skater. III. Series: Sports stories (Toronto, Ont.)

PS8553.A7836S54 2007   jC813'.54   C2007-904969-9

James Lorimer & Co. Ltd,   Distributed in the United States by:
Publishers   Orca Book Publishers
317 Adelaide Street West,   P.O. Box 468
Suite 1002   Custer, WA USA
Toronto, Ontario   98240-0468
M5V 1P9
www.lorimer.ca

Printed and bound in Canada.

CONTENTS

To my parents and all my family,
who encourage me to take risks.

And to Jordan, Alisha, and Naomi, who make
every day more exciting than the next.

Special thanks to Yasir for suggesting the perfect title.

1 Stoked

Jordan Lee stepped into the bright blue world outside his school and dropped his old skateboard to the ground. Without looking, he stopped it from running away with his right foot. His eyes were on the helmet in his hands. The fact that it was as prehistoric as the skateboard was hidden under a layer of stickers from his favourite rock bands, sports teams, and fast-food chains. Jordy scraped off a decaying sticker with his fingernail and flicked it to the ground. He pulled a glow-in-the-dark bandage from the front pocket of his jeans and smiled as he ripped it open and stuck it right on the top. After all the years that he'd been riding, Jordy couldn't even remember the colour of the helmet. The way he figured it, if he was going to be forced to wear a helmet, he might as well make it look cool.

Jordy shoved the helmet over his jet-black hair just as his best friend pushed through the school doors.

"What took you so long, Murph?" Jordy asked.

"Complained to Mr. Jenkins about my English mark."

Jordy shook his head and thought, *who cares about marks? It's June.*

Murphy continued, "I got a B-plus, and the work deserved an A. My presentation had amazing graphics and was loaded with good info."

"Yeah. Who'd have thought that bear fingerprints are just like ours."

Murph grinned proudly. "It's koala bears."

"Murph, you might grow your hair long and adopt the coolest skateboard attitude, but you're still a geek."

"Hey, at least I don't get beaten up on a regular basis anymore!"

Jordy laughed. "Let's get out of here."

The boys jumped on their boards and started riding toward the sidewalk. They were quickly cut off by Carter and Donavan.

"What's up?" asked Carter.

Jordy high-fived Carter. "We were just rolling out."

"To the market?" Donavan asked.

"Where else?"

Jordy watched as Carter snapped the tail of his skateboard down while sliding his front foot forward. At the same time, he jumped in the air and his skateboard followed him like it was glued to his feet.

"Killer ollie," Jordy said, admiring the way that

Carter kept his balance on the board. Sometimes being short could be an advantage.

Carter landed and spun around halfway. "Thanks, Jord. I'm still trying to get a full one-eighty."

Murph leaned in to Jordy and whispered. "What a show-off."

Donavan tugged down the long sleeves of his T-shirt and asked, "Boys, we going to skate or talk?" Donavan had learned to skateboard as a kid on the playgrounds of Punta Cana in the Dominican Republic. He was always complaining that, even in summer, Toronto was too cold.

They all said, "Skate."

Jordy pushed off and followed the boys along the black pavement of the playground. He looked up at the school; it was older than his grandfather. The place had cracks and made weird noises all the time, just like his grandfather.

Suddenly, an ear-splitting shout practically knocked him off his board.

"No skateboarding on school property!"

The boys hopped off their boards, kicked them so the front ends flipped up, and grabbed them with their hands. It was the first trick every skateboard kid learned.

"Sorry Mr. Lamont," Jordy said automatically.

The school caretaker shooed them away with his hands and returned to sweeping.

Seconds off school property, the boys broke out laughing.

"Why'd you apologize to that old goof?" Donavan asked.

Jordy jumped back on his board. "It wasn't a big deal."

"He's not even a teacher. He's just power tripping on you."

Jordy shrugged. "Whatever." He pushed ahead and the others followed him along a sidewalk as two cars tried to rush past a streetcar. Jordy loved gliding around giant cracks in the sidewalk. On his board he felt free from school and his parents. He felt like he could go anywhere.

Carter shouted out, "Want to race?"

Jordy looked over his shoulder and yelled, "Let's just ride." He knew Murph hated to race because he felt he wasn't a good enough skater.

Murph skateboarded up to Jordy. "Let them go if they want to do it."

Carter and Donavan were on Jordy's tail.

Jordy looked at Murph and shook his head in apology. "Where to, Carter?"

Carter grinned. "The usual."

Jordy dug his right shoe into the ground and propelled himself forward. The summer breeze smashed into his face and cooled him off as he dipped into Kensington Market. His quick turn caught Carter and

Donavan by surprise and got Jordy some lead time.

Jordy looked around as he sped through the cramped streets of the Market. He and his board had explored every inch of its deadends and back alleys. He recognized almost every one he saw because they shopped at his parent's produce shop. Jordy flicked his wrist as a hello to a man standing outside a restaurant. When the man turned away, Jordy looked over his shoulder and noticed that Donavan had gained ground, and Carter was hard on Donavan's heels. Not racing but trying to keep up, Murph skateboarded a half-block behind the boys. Jordy bent his knees to lower his centre of gravity and stuck his elbows back like the wings on a fighter jet. He swerved left and right, stopping Donavan from making the pass. He made a sharp right turn and headed toward an older woman. Seeing him coming, she clung to her groceries like her life was about to end and scurried back. Jordy apologized as he passed. He was always apologizing. It bugged him that most people hated skateboarders, especially the way they hogged the sidewalk, but his parents had taught him so well to respect his elders that he still felt guilty enough to say he was sorry.

Jordy shrugged — not an easy thing to do while speeding down the sidewalk. The slight incline of the street was never a big deal to him before, but to a skateboarder it meant burning a lot more energy...

especially on a bad board. His was on its last legs. It was saggy and slow and had seen more street time than they were designed to handle.

He refocused on the race and eyed a rolled-over recycling bin blocking the way. Skateboarding was about chilling on the board, but it was also about pulling off wicked tricks. Jordy lined himself for the jump.

As he approached the blue bin, Jordy realized that he wouldn't get enough height to jump it. He clipped the edge of the bin with the front of his skateboard and rolled head-first into a pile of garbage bags. He hit the bags so hard they ripped open and he was covered in someone's dinner from the night before. He wiped spaghetti off his shirt and looked up as Carter made the jump, followed by Donavan.

Murph hit the brakes. "What's broken? Can you move?"

Jordy nodded slowly. He had wanted to make that jump, but when it came down to it he didn't have what it took to pull it off. He stood up and pulled his skateboard from the wreckage. "Why'd you stop? We can't let them win."

"Well, I calculated my trajectory and velocity… and knew I couldn't make it."

"It's all math to you, isn't it?"

"Yep. My life's too important to leave it to chance."

"I have an idea." Jordy may have bailed on the jump, but he wasn't a quitter.

Murph looked up, "What?"

"Follow me."

Jordy led Murph into an alleyway behind a row of stores.

He smiled at the uncertain look on Murph's face. "Relax. I could find my way around this place if I was blindfolded and spun —"

"I know, I know. Spun around a thousand times."

"And Carter and Donavan couldn't. Follow me."

The alley was lopsided and had enormous puddles. They progressed past brick walls covered with graffiti. Coming out of the alley, they glanced side to side for pedestrians before moving forward.

Murph pointed. "There they are."

Carter and Donavan were moving along at a snail's pace. They were passing a window and laughing at a huge skinned pig hanging in the window of a meat shop.

Jordy couldn't look at it. It wasn't like he was a vegetarian, but he couldn't help thinking that a hanging animal, even a pig, once ran free. He secretly preferred the Disney version of how animals lived.

"Jord, let's race by them. They won't see it coming."

"Don't have to convince me."

Jordy and Murph picked up their boards and crossed the almost empty street. Jordy knew that in an hour the Market would be a zoo.

The boys gathered speed and made their way toward Donavan and Carter. Jordy smirked at the thought of the food chain being reversed — Donavan and Carter strung up in a shop as a bunch of pigs and cows strolled by and laughed at them through the window.

Jordy and Murph whizzed past their friends, catching them off guard. Carter and Donavan stopped laughing at the pig and shot off after them, cutting off pedestrians and flying through stop signs. *They are the kind of people that give skateboarding a worse name that it already has*, Jordy thought.

Jordy and Murphy raced toward the Community Centre. Jordy could see the big red maple leaf appear and disappear as the huge flag out front flapped in the wind.

Jordy looked back. "There's no way they'll catch up, Murph."

"They will if we stop for those people crossing the road."

Jordy didn't have a choice. He pushed down with his back foot until the board scraped against the cement. Murph stopped just behind him.

Donavan and Carter sped by and Jordy watched them head toward the crowd. Donavan bailed at the last minute, but Carter kept going full speed. He crouched down and found an opening between two people as the crowd started to scatter like a flock of pigeons.

By the time Jordy and Murph joined Donavan and reached the Community Centre, Carter had an earlobe-to-earlobe grin plastered on his face. All he said was, "Suckers. Won again."

Donavan sheepishly high-fived him. "Good for you, man. I didn't have the guts."

Jordy and Murph said at the same time, "You got lucky."

"Those who don't have what it takes call it luck. Those who do, call it skill. Raw talent."

Jordy's eyes opened wide and he shrieked, "Watch out, man! One of those people you cut off is coming for you."

Carter craned his neck and turned to look, but there was nobody there.

Jordy got a good laugh, even from Donavan.

Carter growled, "Shut up, Jordy."

"Hey, I didn't tell you to look."

Murph, ever the peacekeeper, said, "Check it out." He was looking through a chain-link fence. They all turned and joined him. Jordy leaned on the fence and gripped his hands on it. "We've waited a long time for this, boys."

Donavan chirped in, "Yeah, it's hard to believe it opens tomorrow."

Carter said, "It's beautiful."

The boys looked at him and laughed.

"What? It is."

Jordy shook his head. "How did we live without this?"

The four boys stared through the fence at the Community Centre's new skateboarding park. Jordy took in the ramps, stairs, ledges — and lots of rails to grind along. In the centre was an amazing bowl. It was deep and it would allow him to get some serious speed and height coming out of it. To Jordy, it was like a mirage, an image of an oasis in the middle of the desert. After months of construction, tomorrow the mirage would transform into a reality.

2 Skateboarding 101

The sun was doing its nightly disappearing act by the time Jordy and Murph were skateboarding home. Their conversation about the new skateboard park was broken up into little chunks as they separated for groups of pedestrians who overflowed out of the market.

"You're late," Murph said.

The boys stopped in front of the produce store owned by Jordy's parents. "Time to feed my brother," Jordy said.

"You say that like he's a dog or something."

"You haven't had to eat dinner with the kid." Jordy picked up his board and held it at his side so his parents couldn't see it. "Later."

Murph sped off and Jordy entered the store. He realized that he didn't have to worry about hiding his board, because the shop was swarming with customers. Like busy bees, they were searching for the cheapest and freshest fruits and veggies for tonight's dinner.

Jordy sidestepped through the crowd toward the counter, where his mother was whipping produce into bags and his father was madly punching in numbers at the cash register. Jordy once timed his dad punch in two hundred prices in a minute. He still had the rolled-up white receipt in his desk drawer to prove it.

Jordy knew that if his parents sold cars, they'd be rich. Unfortunately they sold cantaloupes, avocados, and pomegranates. He watched, amazed, as people scooped up deals from the table of day-olds. He cringed at the thought of eating an over-ripe mushy anything.

His dad looked up from the register. "You're late."

"Sorry."

"Everything okay?"

"Yeah."

His mom looked over from where she stood next to his dad. Jordy always wondered if his mom could bag groceries quicker than his dad could punch in numbers. She glanced at him and said, "No need to hide it. We see your skateboard, Jordan."

His dad read the final total to the customer. "Eight dollars and fifty cents, please," made change for a ten-dollar bill, and said goodbye to the customer in Mandarin. Usually, Jordy would have ducked the customer as she walked past him and ruffled his hair. But she was a repeat customer, so he just let it go.

His mother said. "You better go, your brother is

waiting for you. He's in the —"

"I know. I'm going."

His mom shouted after him. "Dinner's in the fridge. You need to heat it up."

★ ★ ★

At the back of the shop was a glassed-in cool room for some of the more expensive flowers that wouldn't survive the heat outside. Jordy spotted his younger brother, Simon, sitting inside. Jordy could see why Simon liked to hang out in the room in the summer, because it was the only place with air-conditioning. But Simon also liked it because winter was his favourite season, and the room reminded him of the slush, the minus-fifty-degree temperatures, and the chills you get from frequent colds and fevers. That, Jordy didn't get.

"Simon, let's go."

Simon popped up from behind a stack of white lilacs. Jordy hated that he knew they were lilacs.

"Hi, Jordy."

"We're going upstairs."

Simon followed him back into summer and through a side door that led them up the outside stairs.

"You're late," Simon said accusingly.

"So what?"

"Were you skateboarding?"

21

"What else would I be doing?"

The steep narrow steps seemed to take forever to climb. One misstep and they would crash to the bottom — Jordy imagined them tumbling into the empty vegetable crates stacked on the sidewalk. The boys rubbed their shoes clean on a small rug and entered. The first thing Jordy did was open a window to let fresh air in. The air was always stale because the apartment stood empty all day — his parents worked from ten in the morning to ten at night. They even had lunch downstairs.

Simon flopped onto the couch and flipped through channels on the television.

Jordy looked at his little brother. He wanted to slouch on the couch and have someone prepare him dinner. Instead he had to turn on the oven and wait for it to warm up. He sat at the kitchen table and thought about how his life would be easier if his parents bought a microwave. After eight minutes, the red oven light finally blinked on. Jordy stuck the meat into the oven and waited another boring fifteen minutes for it to heat. He considered going into the other room, grabbing the remote from Simon, and watching TV, but he could hear his mother's voice telling him to never leave the stove when it's on.

She would use her serious voice and say, "If you leave with the stove on and forget about it, something could happen and the kitchen could catch fire."

Jordy rubbed his forehead. Every time she reminded him, he had a nightmare of their apartment catching fire. *He tries to put out the fire with a stupid glass of water, but it spreads down the stairs and toward the store. In an instant, burning fruit and customers are running from flaming papayas.* Jordy shook the thought from his mind. He stared at the meat and the red glow surrounding it through the small oven window.

Twenty minutes later, Jordy put the food on two plates. He liked his food mixed together. Simon liked everything separated. Jordy and Simon sat at opposite ends of the kitchen table and ate their meat and rice. Jordy watched as Simon finished all of his meat before touching the rice. The kid had serious problems.

Simon's voice broke the silence. "Do any cool tricks today?"

"Uh-huh."

"Like what?"

"Couple of ollies and a three-sixty."

"All the way around?!"

"Yep." Jordy felt funny bragging about a trick he couldn't do, but what the kid didn't know wouldn't hurt him.

"Wow." Simon grabbed some rice with his chopsticks. "When are you going to show me how to ride?"

"I didn't say I would." Simon's glasses had steamed over from the heat of the meat. Jordy had an idea.

"I'll tell you what. You clean up everything and I'll show you my board."

Jordy watched Simon as he thought about the offer. His little brother wasn't stupid.

"Okay. But just for tonight."

Jordy grabbed his skateboard and put it on the kitchen table. Simon looked at it like it was Tony Hawk's own board.

"Okay, this is the deck." Jordy used a fork to point to the flat wooden platform of the skateboard. "But what you really stand on is the black stuff on top of that. It's called grip tape."

Simon touched the metal below the deck. "What's that?"

"If you let me, I'll get to it."

"Sorry."

Jordy flipped his board onto its side. "Those are trucks."

Simon smiled. "Trucks?"

"That's the name, okay? I didn't make it up." Jordy pointed with the fork again. "The trucks are what keep the wheels attached to the deck. There's also baseplates in between, which are sort of like shock absorbers."

Simon ran his fingers across the wheels and watched them spin.

"Please don't touch the hardware."

Simon tucked his hands under his armpits to stop himself from touching the board.

Jordy continued to tell Simon all about his board. He added some extra tech language to make it more interesting. The way he figured it, he was keeping his little brother entertained and his parents would be happy that he was spending quality time with the kid. More importantly, a few minutes later Jordy was the one on the couch with his feet up and the remote control in his hand. He heard his brother turn on the water to wash the dishes, and then he turned up the volume and smiled.

3 Wipeout

At three-forty-five, Jordy watched the gate to the new skateboard park swing open. He took in a big breath of air and slowly let it out. He had imagined a big ribbon-cutting ceremony. Instead, kids of all kinds just swarmed into the park.

Jordy and his friends crossed the line into the park and watched as skateboarders zipped left and right, performing every trick in the book.

"Wow," was all Murph could say.

"So what do we ... do?" asked Donavan.

Jordy looked at Carter and smiled. "Ride."

Jordy jumped on his board and rolled right into the thick of things. After so many afternoons staring at the park, it felt good to finally feel its slopes and inclines. Up close everything was a lot less intimidating. He saw that only a handful of the kids actually landed their tricks. In a strange way watching other kids wipe out gave him confidence. It was Jordy's turn to go big or go home. All he had to do was pick his move.

Carter whipped by with a big smile on his face. "This place is awesome."

Jordy grinned at him, raring to go. Left foot on the board and right foot dug into the ground, the way a sprinter sets up for a fifty-metre dash, he waited for a gap. When he spotted it, he leaped forward between two boarders. He did a series of figure-eights to loosen up on his way to the centrepiece of the park: the big bowl. It was a lot steeper up close. Playing it safe, he went around it and waited for his turn on its lowest lip.

There was a sixth sense among the skateboarders at the park. No one bumped into each other, everybody waited their turn. Jordy got a nod from a bigger kid — it was his turn at the bowl. He stared down. It had a terrifying vertical drop and he wasn't sure if he could make it up the other end. He needed to take a leap of faith.

Jordy found himself hurtling down the bowl. He leaned forward and held his breath. The steep dive forced him back and low on his board. Air rushed by at the speed of sound. He reached the gully of the bowl and started up the other end even faster. His eyes squinted as he moved from a negative g-force to a positive g. He forced a smile, feeling as though he was riding inside a toilet bowl. The only thing missing was the flush of blue water.

Careening skyward, Jordy had no time to figure

out what to do once he was airborne. He changed his position on the deck, leaning forward so he wouldn't fall backward. He didn't look back and he didn't look up — he just stared at his feet. When he passed the lip of the bowl and his skateboard was no longer connected to the earth, he wished the ride was over. Looking down now meant he was looking at how high he was climbing.

His hang-time lasted forever before gravity started to work its magic. Jordy thought, *there is no way my board can handle the impact*. The highest it had been was over a curb, and even then it wobbled and creaked. His only option was to bail. Crashing back to earth, he pushed his board away. He landed hard on his feet and then rolled to his knees. Like a living thing, his skateboard thrashed around worse than a fish out of water.

Murphy and Donavan approached, their eyes wide open.

Murph leaned down next to Jordy. "Okay, just tell me what's broken."

Jordy looked up. "Would you stop saying that?!"

Murph spoke louder. "Can you move your feet?"

"I'm okay, Murph."

"Just get up slowly."

Murph held out his hand, but Jordy bounced up on his own, relieved to be alive. "That was so cool!"

"I have to try that. Got any advice?" Donavan asked.

Jordy thought about it and came up with nothing. "Uh, just keep low."

"Thanks." Donavan shot off.

Jordy felt the adrenaline still ripping through his veins. "Murph, you have to do the bowl."

Murph took a long hard look at the bowl and then shook his head side to side. "If I can't control my velocity, I can't control my rate of descent. And if I can't do that —"

Jordy cut him off. "Okay, okay. You're ruining my buzz."

Carter swung by, screeching to a halt centimetres from Jordy. "You land the bowl?"

"Almost. I collected some serious air miles."

Carter smiled. "I just landed a one-eighty over a ramp. I love this place."

Jordy smirked back, "Too bad they don't have people walking through."

"What do you mean?"

"I thought you'd miss running over pedestrians." That got a laugh, even from Carter. But Jordy was a little jealous. Not only could Carter pull off great tricks, but he looked cool on his new board.

Carter held his right hand up and Jordy and Murph high-fived him. "Where's D?"

Jordy turned and pointed to Donavan flying out of the big bowl.

Murph turned away, "I can't watch this."

Donavan knelt on his board and held onto it with his right hand. He let go just before impact, and managed to land.

Jordy watched him bounce off his board, and still stop on his feet. Jordy knew that, if he did it a few times, he could master it. He remembered that Murph told him to start off slow, but where would that get him? The skateboarder code was to push the envelope.

Carter sped toward Donavan and congratulated him by banging their helmets together.

Jordy turned to Murph. "I need to get some grip tape. My feet aren't sticking to the board."

"Right, it's definitely the grip tape." Murph paused before he said, "Don't let Carter get to you."

"You're right."

"I am? Yes, I am."

"What I need to do is figure out how to come out the other end of the bowl with a one-eighty."

"Okay?"

"Let's roll."

Moving through the park, Jordy repaired his confidence by pushing down on the back of his board until the front wheels lifted up.

Murph followed. "Nice manual."

"Thanks."

Jordy lowered his board as he approached the section of the park that had a series of mini hills. He watched Murph do a rolling kickflip, jumping with the board and letting it spin in the air before landing. Murph pointed to the mini hills, "Let's do that."

Jordy followed Murph. The boys took the hills fast, springing up and down repeatedly.

"I feel a little seasick, Murph."

"Me too. Want to do it again?"

"Yeah."

Coming out of the last hill, Jordy rode fakie, turning his body so it looked like he was going backward while moving forward. His confidence was now completely refuelled. He held his arm out in front of Murph.

"What's wrong?" Murph asked, stopping beside him.

Jordy nodded in the direction of a long cement rail. It was knee high, and had a flat wide top.

"I have to do it."

"You have to get your ollie down before you do that."

"The only way for me to get my ollie down is to keep doing that until I get it. Remind me what to do again."

"If your parents knew I was encouraging you, they'd kill me."

"Whatever."

Murph held his thumb up in the air like a surveyor. "Okay. Looks just under forty degrees. Your speed needs to be ..."

"Forget it. I'm going for it."

"You're pushing your luck."

"If you can do it, I can do it." Jordy smiled. "No offence."

"None taken. Now let me walk you through it."

"That doesn't work for me. There comes a time in every kid's life when he has to just do it."

"There's come a time in every kid's life when he says, 'Why'd I do that and why was I so stupid?'"

Jordy chuckled, keeping his eyes on his target.

Murph wasn't done yet. "Break your leg, and there goes my summer. Don't be selfish."

"The glass is always half-empty with you."

"I'm going to get help."

Jordy had stopped listening. "Uh-huh."

"You want a private room on the ward?"

Jordy's old trucks began to spin. He picked up as much speed as he could before reaching the go/no-go point. He was going. He kicked the back of his board to get height — and he went airborne. Problem was, his skateboard didn't. Out of the corner of his eye, he saw someone skateboard in front of him. He tried to land away from the person as he barrel-rolled out of control. His legs clipped the skateboarder as he went down.

Jordy got to his feet and saw a girl on the ground. She sat with her arms crossed over her knees.

Embarrassed and concerned, Jordy asked if she was okay.

She got to her feet and picked up her board. It had bright pink trucks and wheels, the bright colour making them stand out from under the black deck.

"I've been worse. You have to keep your head up."

"I know. I'm sorry I just …"

"No, you have to keep your head up."

"I said I was sorry."

She smiled. "I mean it's why you're not making the trick."

She got on her skateboard and sped off.

He just stared at her as she rode up a short ramp and spun around in the air, her hand holding the end of her board. *Good tailgrab*, he thought.

Murph, Donavan, and Carter ran up. They tried not to snicker along with the other skateboarders who had grouped in their vicinity.

Carter did the unnecessary recap. "You blindsided her."

Donavan couldn't hold in his laugh. "There are easier ways to get a girl's number."

Murph was silent. They both knew that an, "I told you so," would be redundant.

A high-school–aged skateboarder stepped out from the crowd and said, "Nice brainbucket!"

Jordy looked at him, confused.

Carter piped in. "He's talking about your whack helmet."

The snide comments were interrupted as a

community worker stood on the upper lip of the bowl and blew his whistle to get everyone's attention.

"Boys and girls." He was tall and slender. The sun gleamed off his bald head. "Welcome to the Kensington Market Skateboard Park."

Donavan turned to his friends and asked, "Who's this guy?"

"I think he's about to tell us," Murph assumed.

"My name's Mr. Blight."

Murph eyed Donavan.

"I'm the lead community worker at the Centre. I hope you are enjoying the skateboarding park."

Understatement of the year, Jordy thought.

Mr. Blight waited for everyone to stop talking. "Okay, we need to go over the Park rules, and then I have a special announcement." He cleared his throat. "There are five rules that everyone needs to follow. First, everyone needs to respect other skateboarders. We all need to share ..."

Jordy tuned out the rest of Mr. Blight's *blah-blah-blah*. He turned his head and whispered to Carter, "The only rule is that there are no rules."

Carter nodded his head and butted knuckles with Jordy.

Jordy's eyes focused on Mr. Blight's head. It was so perfectly shaven it reflected the sun, making a big bright spot that seemed to fill his vision.

Mr. Clean wrapped up his list of rules. "By the way,

people, these rules are posted at the gate when you enter. Please take the time to read them over."

Jordy turned to Murph, "And the number one way to lose us …"

Murph completed Jordy's thought, "Is to call us *people.*"

But even Jordy listened after Mr. Clean's next sentence: "Here's the big announcement. We're having a skateboarding competition next month."

The entire park fell silent. Mr. Clean said, "It's going to be a two-day competition. Start practising your routines. I'm doing the judging with a special guest. Prizes are gift certificates to Kumani's Sports Store down the street. Third place gets fifty, second gets a hundred, and first gets a hundred and fifty dollars' worth. Sign-up's inside."

The crowd went ballistic.

Jordy turned to the boys, "I can get a new skateboard!"

Carter tapped his skateboard. "Only if you win, buddy. You're going to need all the luck you can get … I could use a backup board."

★ ★ ★

Jordy was bursting with excitement. He could hardly stay on his skateboard on the way home. He turned to Murph. "You okay?"

"Yeah."

"Then why aren't you jumping up and down?"

Jordy and Murph always told each other every-thing, even private stuff — like when Murph's parents were talking about getting a divorce, or when Jordy's family's store almost went bankrupt.

"Because I don't stand a chance of winning."

"Yeah, right. You have amazing balance. You can pull off tricks I can't. You just have to be confident."

"Guess so."

"We'll help each other."

"Okay."

Jordy hopped sideways off his board and stopped it with his foot.

Murph caught on and stopped. "What now?"

Jordy was staring at a park bench.

"Come on, man, it's late, " said Murph.

"If I'm going to place top-ten, I have to be able to ride a stupid bench."

"Do I have to remind you what happened when you tried the rail?"

All of Jordy's attention was on the bench. "If I can get the right velocity and angles …"

Murph laughed. "I thought that doesn't work for you."

"Murph, you don't understand. I want to win it."

Before Murph could respond, Jordy was on his way.

Jordy rolled along the sidewalk, gaining speed with the passing of every crack. He adjusted his direction slightly by shifting his hips. As he saw the bench approach, he slammed his foot down on the back of his board. In a flash, he rocketed into the air. Suddenly, he heard in his head the voice of the skater girl: "Keep your head up." He lifted his head and kept the bench in his sights. His wheels touched down on the bench and he glided across it. He jumped off the other side and landed without a glitch.

"You did it!" Murph shouted.

Jordy bounced up and down like a crazy rubber ball.

"That was incredible!" said Murph. "I thought I would have to wipe you off the sidewalk."

"I've got to do that again."

"Actually, you have to get home and feed your brother. You'll be lucky if he hasn't keeled over from starvation. "

Jordy smiled. His mind was only on winning the competition.

4 Skater Girl

Jordy and Murph carried their orange lunch trays through the cafeteria and sat across from Carter and Donavan.

Carter said around a mouthful of turkey sandwich, "There's the man!"

Jordy looked away. He knew they were going to launch into him about his performance the day before.

Carter swallowed his food and then took another big bite. "That was seriously the sweetest pickup move ever."

Jordy looked at Murph and then to Donavan. "What's this guy on?"

Ignoring Jordy's confusion, Donavan said, "Yeah, you picked her right up off the ground!" Carter and Donavan laughed hysterically.

Jordy shrugged them off, but there was no way they were stopping. *Their one-liners are always so rehearsed*, Jordy thought.

"Come on, Murph," Carter said. "Why aren't you laughing? Not only was it one of the worst wipeouts, it was also one of the worst skater-girl pickups ever."

"It's not that funny."

"*It's not that funny*," Carter mocked in a goofy voice.

Jordy cringed when he saw a piece of turkey fly from Carter's mouth and land on Murph's shirt.

Murph looked down. He flicked the piece of turkey with his finger and it hit Donavan in the face.

Donavan stopped laughing when the piece of turkey hit his forehead and just stuck there.

Jordy, Murph, and even Carter looked over and started laughing. Donavan used both hands to wipe the turkey fragment off him, as though it was a poisonous spider.

Jordy high-fived Murph, proud that his best friend finally zinged one of the jokers.

★ ★ ★

Jordy could almost smell the end of school; at least he could count the school days left on his fingers. He entered the skateboarding park with Murph in tow.

Murph asked, "I don't get why you just sat there at lunch."

"What am I suppose to do?"

"I don't know. Defend yourself. Fight back. Something."

Jordy's eyes scanned the park. "Guess so," he said, zoned out.

Murph tapped on Jordy's helmet. "Hello, anyone home?"

Jordy tilted his head away. "Murph, can we just skate?"

Murph shook his head as though he had come to a big realization.

Jordy noticed. "What now?"

"How could I have been so stupid? You *are* thinking about that skater girl."

"No, I'm not. No way."

"It's the only thing that makes sense."

"Okay, Murph. I swear that's not it. I don't like her. It's just that I finally made it up and over that park bench because of what she said."

"What did she say?"

"To keep my head up."

"Wow. I'm blown away by her insight."

"No, it's a big deal. I was staring down at my board. No wonder I couldn't make the trick."

Murph chewed on his bottom lip. "I could have told you that."

"But you didn't. She did."

"So you like her, but you don't like her."

"No, Murph. I'm just wondering what else I can pick up from her."

"Like lessons."

"No, no. If I'm gonna win the competition, I need to get better by riding with a rider who's much better than me."

"I'll ignore the fact that you just insulted my skateboard skills … but I get it." Murph said with a smirk. "But you do have a problem."

"What's that?"

"I don't think she goes to our school and you don't know her name."

"But she does ride at this park. So keep an eye out for her."

"Okay."

Jordy and Murph stepped on their boards.

"One more thing, Murph. The boys don't know about this. Okay?"

"Don't know about what?" Carter and Donavan approached from behind them.

Time to put Carter and Donavan in their place, thought Jordy. He pushed forward and sped away on his board. He hit a ramp, lifted the front end of his board, and almost lost his balance. *Just focus*, he told himself. He rounded back and lined up with the rail. As he gained speed, he kept his head up and pointed at the target. He pushed down on his board, and then jumped up into the air. Like a trained dog, his board followed him as he landed on the rail. He rode it and then pushed off it into a soft landing.

Jordy tried to hide the fact that he was out of

breath, while Carter and Donavan gave him a round of over-the-top applause.

"Wow, Jordo, you just might give me a run for my money," said Carter.

"*Your* money?" Jordy shook his head.

"But you know what? Second place is respectable!"

Donavan piped in, "Hey, second place is my spot."

Carter flicked his hand. "Third, whatever, same thing."

Donavan looked at Carter.

"You know, Carter," Murph said, "you have a way with words."

Jordy had had enough. "Time to ride."

Before speeding off with Murph, he asked Donavan if he wanted to join them.

Donavan paused a moment before turning to follow Carter.

Jordy and Murph climbed the stairs of the vertical ramp. From there they could see most of the park.

"Ready, Jord?"

"In a sec." Jordy scanned the horizon for the skater girl. He couldn't spot her pink trucks and wheels. "Yeah, let's go."

Both boys inched forward and let the ramp take care of the rest. They dipped down and raced off the ramp at top speed.

Jordy noticed kids the size of his brother try monster tricks they obviously couldn't pull off. A few on-duty community workers walked around with walkie-talkies. Jordy figured, *if any of these kids break a leg, someone has to be there to help.* The park quickly became flooded with skateboarders again and he gave up on finding the skater girl.

★ ★ ★

Jordy's mom and dad smiled when Jordy entered the store. He knew they were happy to see him arrive on time.

His mom gave him a hug and told him she really appreciated him making an effort. Then she took a second look. "Are you okay?"

"I'm fine, Mom."

"You look a little stressed. Is it school?"

"It's definitely not school. Trust me."

Jordy walked toward the cold room. He opened the door and was hit with a breeze that reminded him of parkas and Christmas trees. He could sort of see why his brother enjoyed this place. Jordy called out to his brother.

Simon popped out from underneath a shelf.

"Let's go." Jordy led his brother out of the cold room and toward the door to get upstairs.

Their mom shouted, in the middle of helping a customer, "Make sure to stir the noodles."

Jordy nodded. Then something caught his eye.

Skater girl. She passed by the shop window.

He cut off a customer on his way to the counter and made a run for the door. Despite protests from his mom and dad, he shot outside.

The sidewalk was crowded and he had lost sight of her. As he ran, slaloming between strangers, he caught a glimpse of her over a woman's shoulder. He reached her as she entered a clothing store.

"Hey."

She turned. "Hi, wipeout boy." When she saw the look on his face, she hurried to say, "I'm just kidding. What's up?"

"I was, uh …" He pointed to the clothing store. "Going shopping?"

"Well this is my store, my parent's store."

"Oh." He looked up at the sign: *Harriet's Used Clothing Depot.* In the window, second-hand jeans and T-shirts were hanging.

"My family owns the fruit and vegetable store down the road — Kensington Produce."

"The one that sells the dragon fruit? I'm in there all the time. How come I never saw you?

"I was probably babysitting my brother upstairs."

"Cool. So again, what's up?"

"I was just wondering if you wanted to go, ah, skateboarding sometime?"

"You're cute but, sorry, I'm not interested."

"No, no, I didn't mean like that."

"Then what did you mean?"

"Just … you helped me with a trick I couldn't do before."

"You mean the heads-up thing? That was nothing."

"Yeah, but it worked." For the first time in the conversation Jordy breathed. "So, I was just wondering if you wanted to go skateboarding some time. Just skateboarding."

He watched as she thought about it, scratching the side of her head with a fingernail painted with a pink stripe. She nodded. "Sure, why not."

"Great. How about tomorrow after school?"

"Okay."

She was about to go. "Your name's not Harriet is it?"

"No, that's my mom."

Jordy was relieved. A name like Harriet was just not right for a skater girl.

"I'm Alisha … Ali."

"Okay." Jordy turned to leave.

"Hey, what's your name?"

"Oh, sorry. Jordan … Jordy."

"Okay, Jordy, see you tomorrow." She turned and said over her shoulder, "And if you can, bring some dragon fruit."

5 Cement Surfing

The next day Jordy met Ali outside her parents' store. He carried his skateboard, his helmet, and a white plastic bag filled with dragon fruit.

Ali flew out of the entrance, bounced down the five stairs, and stopped on the sidewalk. "Hi, Jordy."

"Hi." He held out his bag of dragon fruit to her.

"Okay, wow. Did you leave any for the store?"

He laughed as she threw the fruit into her brown messenger bag and they started to ride.

"What do you think of the skate park?" he asked.

"It's all right. I prefer riding around the Market."

"What about the ramps and the rails and the … you know?"

"You can get all of that right here." She pointed. "Jumping that fire hydrant is a lot harder than anything you'll find at that park."

"Yeah, but that bowl is pretty impressive."

"That's true. What I like about it out here is that

you have to be flexible. You have to deal with the unexpected."

Jordy nodded in agreement. He kept one eye on where they were going and the other on Ali's skateboard and what she was doing with it. While she talked, she pulled off an effortless kickflip over divots on the sidewalk.

"Heads up over there."

He looked up and saw that his part of the sidewalk turned into a sewer grate. He tried to kickflip over it, but he couldn't land it.

"Try placing your feet on the edge of one side of the board." She did it herself. "That way the board spins straight up and straight down."

"I can do it." Jordy jumped off his board and picked it up. He flicked the two back wheels with his fingers. "It's just my wheels. They're sticking."

"I've seen worse."

Jordy held his board up to her and spun the wheels again. She looked carefully at them, but didn't say anything.

"What?" he asked.

"Nothing."

Jordy got back on his board. They continued through a crosswalk and to the edge of Kensington Market, where the stores stopped and the houses began. There was hardly any traffic, so they moved from the sidewalk to the street.

He noticed that her pink ankle-high shoes matched the pink on her board. "So how long have your parents had the store?"

"Since before I was born. They always talk about selling it but they never do."

"They don't like it?"

"They hate the hours."

"Yeah, my parents work almost every weekend."

They slowed down at a four-way stop. There were no cars in sight, so they continued through.

Jordy checked out the rows of houses with small front lawns. "These are nice," he said. "I'd love to live here."

"Who wouldn't?"

They turned left and were passed by a few cyclists.

"Did you sign up for the competition?" asked Jordy.

"Some of my friends talked me into it," Ali replied.

"I'm hoping to win so I can get a new skateboard."

"I think if you regrip yours, and tighten or change the struts, it could be a lot better."

"Yeah, but there's a great board I've already picked out. It's got yellow and red flames on top. The struts and wheels glow in the dark."

"Sounds expensive."

"The guy said if I win he'd give me the display board for one-fifty."

"So you've got it all worked out."

"Yeah, but I actually think you're gonna win."

"Really?"

"You're a great skateboarder."

"Hey, follow me. These are fun."

Ali turned onto a street that had speed bumps. She took the first one at a good speed and, when she was in the air, she did a one-eighty, spinning so she landed moving forward but facing backward.

"Try a one-eighty."

Jordy's right foot pushed against the ground, and then he put it back on the board and jumped the speed bump. He twisted his body in the air, but he couldn't make the full turn. He bailed, grabbed his board, and continued down the street like nothing happened.

Ali hit the next speed bump facing backward and did another one-eighty in the air, this time landing facing forward. "Keep your hands out so you can keep your balance."

This time, as Jordy's wheels hit the cement bump, he kept his head up, extended his arms, and twisted his upper body. On his way down he felt the skateboard below his shoes. It was facing the right way! He made a soft landing and kept rolling.

"Nice one," Ali said approvingly.

Jordy was all smiles. Inviting Ali to skate was the best decision of his life. For what he had picked up in less than an hour, it was worth emptying his parent's store of dragon fruit.

"Remember what I said about expecting the unexpected?"

"Yeah."

"That blue car up ahead is backing out of the driveway!"

Jordy whipped his back foot off his board and dragged it across the ground until he stopped.

He looked sideways and admired the way Ali stopped by doing a heel drag. She lifted one foot and placed its heel so it was sticking off the back of her skateboard. Then she leaned back so the front of her board lifted off the ground.

He stored the image so he could practise the move later. He figured if he could lift the front of his board up in a manual, he could do it in a stop like she did.

The car blindly backed out of the driveway as Ali yelled at the driver. Talking on his cell phone, the driver couldn't hear a thing.

"That guy needs to learn to keep his head up," Jordy joked.

"We should probably circle back toward the Market."

"Sure."

★ ★ ★

On the steps in front of Harriet's Used Clothing Depot, Ali pulled a screwdriver and wrench from her dad's toolbox. She tightened the struts and wheels on Jordy's board.

"You're right, this is ancient. Was it your grandfather's?"

"Actually my grandfather never ..."

"That was a joke."

"Oh." Jordy let out a quick laugh.

"Come here. Hold this."

Jordy gripped the wrench.

"Tighten it around that and hold it."

Jordy slid the wrench around a nut that held the wheel to the strut. He watched Ali hard at work on his skateboard.

"This should make the ride a little smoother and the board a little less wobbly."

As she spoke, he had problems concentrating. He found himself checking her out. He couldn't stop himself. Up until now he hadn't noticed her wavy hair that flowed from under her helmet. He looked away, not wanting to get caught staring. His eyes drifted up her black tights and denim miniskirt to her purple T-shirt.

"You can let go." Her voice startled him.

He looked down and realized he still had the wrench in position.

"Sorry."

"So what do you think?"

He picked up his board and rolled the wheels with his fingers. "It's perfect. Thanks a lot, Ali."

"No problem."

"So how'd you get into skateboarding?"

"You're going to laugh."

"Probably."

"Okay. A customer forgot a skateboard in the changing room at the store. We didn't know whose it was, and waited for over two weeks, but the board's owner never came back for it."

"That's bizarre."

"I was just a kid, so I use to sit on it and move around the store. It took a while before I actually stood on it."

"Okay, but how did you get so great?"

She blushed. "I was starting to get in the way of customers, so I went into the basement. I spent all my time down there, just me and the boxes of used jeans. It took a while before I hit the streets. And I wouldn't say I'm great."

"Cool."

"I love the sport … always have."

"Me too. And it's not about anything else but being on the board and riding."

"Exactly."

"And winning the competition."

"Exactly!"

Ali unsnapped the messenger bag from her shoulder and pulled out a dragon fruit. It was round and pink with scales. "Thanks. I don't know how I'll ever finish them."

"Give them to your parents."

"I'm the only one that likes them. Besides, I don't want to waste them."

"Oh."

She kept a few and put the rest back into the plastic bag. As she handed them to Jordy, she said, "Tomorrow, just bring a couple." She disappeared into the store.

Jordy boarded home. The skateboard felt a lot better, but he was confused. He had a good time and picked up some good skills, but he didn't get why he couldn't get his mind off her. He couldn't shake Ali from his thoughts.

When Jordy got to the store, he dumped the dragon fruit in their rightful spot while his parents weren't looking. He took his little brother upstairs and fed him without complaint. His mind was locked on skateboarding and Ali. After washing the dishes, he watched TV with his brother until his parents closed the shop and came upstairs.

They were surprised to find two plates of food waiting for them in the kitchen. It was enough to make up for Jordy running out of the store. Even his dad was happy.

After supper, Jordy washed their dishes. His parents were even more elated — and more than a little suspicious. His mom looked at him like something was up. In one day, he had gone from feeling down to feeling sky high. Jordy excused himself to his bedroom.

The room was small, but Jordy really didn't need more space. There was space for his bed and a small pine desk with a shelf above it. On the wall behind his bed was a cutout picture of a sleek black skateboard. It was called the Eliminator, and it was his dream board. With it, he knew he could conquer anything. On the shelf above his desk were copies of *Skateboarder* magazine and a few framed pictures of his family. One photo was taken the day his parents surprised him by giving him his skateboard. They had finally caved into Jordy's persistent requests. Jordy smiled at the irony — they had given him the skateboard that they hated him riding.

With the door closed, this was Jordy's private world. No one was judging him, hassling him, or yelling at him. He turned on his CD player and turned to track 8, his favourite. The song was half rap, half rant. It was a song created for skateboarders.

Jordy grabbed his skateboard and dropped it on the green shag carpet. He jumped on it, leaned back, and balanced on the back wheels. He knew he had to improve his balance if he was going to do tricks while flying through the air. He held the wheelie for the rest of the song, the carpet gripping the wheels tight.

When the song faded into the next one, he dropped the board and moved so the back of his feet were hanging off the side the way Ali's did. He held his balance and, with his arms out, he kicked the board down and jumped up so it flipped underneath him in the air. It rotated once and landed on its wheels, just as his feet gripped the deck.

He felt his landing send shock waves throughout the building. He turned up the music to cover the noise, even though he knew his parents worked so hard they could sleep through an earthquake. He didn't have to worry about the noise echoing downstairs, because the store was closed. The worst thing that could happen was the fruit and veggies would roll around in their stands.

Jordy repeated the trick until he could do it with his eyes closed. Exhausted, he turned down the music and flopped down on his bed. He knew trying to sleep would be futile; he couldn't get his mind off Ali.

6 The Hangout

The school day was almost over. When Jordy went to write his homework in his agenda, he found that his only pencil, the one he had brought to school after March break, was too dull to write with. He had sharpened it so much that all that was left was a stub. The eraser was longer than the pencil. Jordy stood up and took it to the pencil sharpener. He put it inside and pinched on the eraser so he wouldn't lose it. The blade spun as he cranked it, and Jordy realized that it wasn't grabbing the pencil. He pushed it in as far as he could while turning the handle. He felt the crank stop suddenly and realized that he was no longer holding onto the pencil.

"Jordy, what are you doing there?"

He turned to see Mr. Fletcher staring at him, his hands pressed on his hips. "Sharpening my pencil."

Mr. Fletcher adjusted his glasses and asked, "What pencil?"

"Well …"

The teacher signalled for Jordy to have a seat.

The desks were arranged in groups, and Jordy sat next to Murph. Before Jordy could ask, Murph whipped out a blue mechanical pencil, clicked down on it twice, and handed it to him.

"Thanks."

Jordy scribbled down the homework for the night. It was easy June stuff — read for thirty minutes and review fractions.

Murph whispered, "Want to come over after school?"

"Ahhh."

"We can play my Tony Hawk video game."

"Can't."

"Seeing her?"

Jordy nodded. He could see a sour expression storm across Murph's face. "Hey, I already told her I'd meet her."

Murph nodded. "But it's pouring out. Kind of hard to go skateboarding."

Jordy looked up and saw rain beating down on the classroom window.

Jordy thought, *it's just one stupid afternoon.* He said, "But I can't call and cancel. I don't have her number."

"So where are you meeting her?"

"In front of her parents' store."

"Oh. Okay."

Murph carefully wrote down the rest of his homework. Jordy could tell he was peeved. Before he could say anything, Murph jumped in.

"So it's not just about skateboarding, then?"

"Look, all I know is we have plans. It could easily stop raining."

Jordy wondered why he didn't know what to say to Murph anymore. Fortunately it was time to stack chairs before the bell rang.

Jordy twirled his locker combination, left, right, then left again, and swung it open. It was stuffed bottom to top, filled with bits and pieces that had built up over the school year.

Murph peeked in and smirked. His locker was September clean.

Carter and Donavan walked over, clanging their skateboards against a series of closed lockers.

They were the last people Jordy wanted to deal with.

"We missed you the last couple days," Carter said.

Jordy racked his brain for a way to change the conversation. All that popped up were lame excuses. He chose the most believable one. "I was helping my dad at the store."

Carter asked, "And what about Little Miss Skater Girl?"

"What about her?" Jordy shot a look at Murph.

In Carter and Donavan's tag team, it was Donavan's

turn to tighten the grip on Jordy. "You're in love with her, so we figure you were with her."

Jordy couldn't believe that the teasing was getting under his skin. Maybe it was because of the way they were talking about Ali. Jordy was used to Carter and Donavan having way too much fun baiting him, but all Ali was doing was showing him a few tricks. The only rescue from the situation would be to win the stupid tournament. That would shut his friends up for good. He slammed his locker closed and started walking away.

"Hey, Jordy. Wanna go riding now?" Carter's voice followed him down the hall.

Jordy couldn't come up with another excuse. Then he realized he didn't have to. "It's raining outside."

As Jordy walked, the cold rain droplets felt good on his face. He thought about how badly he wanted to win the tournament and why. He wasn't just playing for a new skateboard now; he wanted to have something to hold over Carter and Donavan. If Ali could teach him some more tricks, and he won it, even Murph would understand.

Jordy took shelter on the steps of Harriet's Used Clothing Depot. A canvas canopy bulged above his head, filled with water. He watched as some of it seeped over the edges and splattered on the ground.

Ali stepped down onto the stairs. Jordy watched her hold her hand out to cup rainwater.

"We can't go skateboarding, but I still love the rain." She spread her fingers apart and let the water trickle down to the ground.

The competition was two weeks away, and Jordy couldn't afford to miss a day of practice. He was about to say that the rain might stop, but a big clash of thunder shook the Market.

"We could always go skateboarding another day."

Jordy nodded, but what he was really trying to do was think of an idea. He opened his knapsack and pulled out another white bag holding two dragon fruit. Silently, he handed them to Ali.

"Thanks," she said. She handed one back to him and they both sat on the steps.

He took a bite and asked, "Do you have a routine planned for the tournament?"

"Yeah, but I hate to use it."

"Why?"

"Because you have to run on your instinct. That's what separates the top from the bottom. Some go out there and stick to what they practised. The good ones are flexible and mix things up on the fly."

"They mix it up."

"Yeah."

Jordy thought, *if that's the only tip I get from her, it's still enough to give me a shot at the top spot.*

"Do you have a routine?" Ali asked.

"I'm working on it. I want to make it right for the

skate park." He was staring out beyond the canopy.

"What are you looking at?"

"Let's go skateboarding."

"What?"

"Trust me."

Ali followed Jordy across the street and through an alley that came out in front of a five-storey parking garage. They entered through two big green doors and ran up the damp stairwell. Except for the bottom two floors, the garage was deserted.

Jordy looked up as the top floor of the garage opened to an amazing skyline view of the city. Through the beads of pouring rain they could see the CN Tower sticking up from the jagged outline of the tall downtown buildings.

Jordy and Ali skateboarded around the empty space, weaving in and out of the huge pillars that held the structure together. He watched as she effortlessly moved side to side to keep the skateboard moving, and injected extra speed before a turn by lowering her foot just above the ground and pushing forward repeatedly.

At the end of two laps around the lot, she asked him if he wanted to race. "Just for fun," she said.

They lined up on opposite sides of the parking lot. A steep ramp heading down to the next floor separated them.

She cupped her hands in front of her mouth and shouted, "Three, two …"

On *one*, Jordy dug his right foot down and propelled himself forward. In sprint mode, he kept pushing forward, keeping the skateboard on track with his left foot. As a giant pillar approached, he flew around it, holding his hands up and sucking in his body so he didn't hit it with flailing arms or legs. Once past the pillar, he dropped his hands and grinded, pushing his foot into the ground to regain the speed he lost in the turn. He passed so close to the next pillar, he felt his T-shirt wipe against it. Another two pillars and the finish line was in sight. He looked over at Ali, who was two skateboard-lengths behind him. He crossed the last yellow parking line, did a long arc-shaped turn, and stopped close to her.

"You are fast," she said between gulps of air.

"Actually, I didn't know I was that fast." Jordy's legs were in pain, but he wanted to go again.

Ali's hands were down on her knees as her body sighed up and down. "This place is great."

"It's like our own private park."

She stood upright and asked, "Do you know how to do a drop-in?"

"No."

"You're going to need it for the competition."

"What is it?"

"I'll show you." She looked around until she spotted something. "Follow me."

They rode toward the top of the ramp that led

down to the next level.

Jordy looked down. His mind was suddenly full of his horrible experience riding the giant bowl at the skateboard park.

"When you're going down a ramp or into a bowl, you get extra points for dropping in," Ali was explaining.

"Yeah, at the skate park I sort of jumped into the bowl and it spat me out the other side."

"That's because you didn't do this." Ali aligned herself with the top of the ramp just before the drop. She pushed down on the tail of the skateboard so the deck pointed up, leaving her front wheels dangling in the air.

She smiled. "Here's the cool part." Ali kept one foot on the tail and put the other over the front trucks of her skateboard. She was suspended in air.

"I can't do that," Jordy protested.

"Come on, give it a shot. You've got nothing to lose — and the best part is that nobody is watching."

"Except you."

She turned her head away. "Tell me when you're on it."

Jordy made every move with exacting precision. Back foot down holding down the back of the board — check. Front of the board out in the air over the drop — check. He raised his front foot and slowly placed it on his board. As soon as his foot made contact, the board shot down. Jordy torpedoed down the ramp and yelped.

He was going as fast as he had ever gone on his skateboard. He could feel the trucks and wheels vibrate madly. He tried to think of what to do next as wet air pushed against his face and the bottom of the ramp approached. All he could do was imagine himself bursting over the side of the parking lot.

From somewhere behind him, he heard Ali shout, "Turn right!"

His stomach dropped when he hit the bottom of the ramp and levelled off. He bent down and leaned right, veering away from the side of the building and toward safety. As he slowed down, he dropped his foot off the board to create friction with the ground.

Ali was right behind him. "Are you okay?"

"That was awesome. Scary — but what a rush!"

"I seriously thought you were going off the edge of the building."

"I wasn't that out of control." He knew he almost had been, but he wasn't going to admit it. Jordy lifted his helmet and wiped the cold sweat that had formed above his forehead. "So that's dropping in."

"Pretty much. The only difference is you weren't supposed to drop yet."

"Oh."

"Want to try it again?"

"Why not?"

As they climbed the ramp, he relived every terrifying second in his mind.

He watched Ali put her board into position. She placed her front foot on the board and stood, suspended in air. "I probably should have told you to really press down hard with your back foot."

He smiled. "That would have been nice."

She smiled back. "Sorry."

He wiped away more sweat with the back of his hand and lifted his front foot. The board began to wobble, so he pressed really hard on it with his back foot. He lightly placed his front foot on the board. He was balanced over the lip of the ramp! It felt weird to know that there was nothing but air below.

Ali said, "That'll get you points."

"Great. Now what?"

"Just enjoy hanging there. The feeling that you're going to fall down is all in your head."

"Cool." He looked around, trying to ignore the steep drop right below him. After he took in the scenery he said, "Seriously, now what?"

"There's no turning back now. Once you're up on it you have to go for it."

"Translate that for me, please."

"Stomp down on the board with your front foot and let gravity take care of the rest."

"Okay, here I go."

"Wait."

He looked up.

"Let's go down two levels."

"You're crazy." Jordy lifted his left foot and said, "Last one down has to carry the other person's board back up." He stomped down on the board. As soon as the front wheels touched ground, he went from zero to thirty in five seconds.

He took a quick glance back and saw Ali hot on his tail. He smiled and focused on the ramp as it unfolded at lightning speed. What a great ride! When he rolled out on the bottom, he swerved right. Out of the corner of his eye, he saw Ali swerve left. She was giving him a run for his money, pushing him to ride better than he had ever done before.

7 Boiling Point

Jordy's face tightened and he felt like it might explode.

Ali was concerned, but she was also smiling. "Should I call 911?"

"No, it's okay." Jordy put his hands over his face. "Just brain freeze."

She held in her laugh as he slowly recovered from the last of his orange slush.

"I'm okay now."

It was Pedestrian Sunday at Kensington Market, and people flooded the streets. Jordy felt bad that his parents were stuck inside the shop working. They were convinced that shoppers would stop in, even though Jordy told them that all they were looking for was cheap deals on clothes and antiques.

He and Ali sat on a park bench with their feet on the perfect foot rests, their skateboards.

Jordy knocked his knuckles on the bench and said, "Hard to believe that, just a week ago, I couldn't jump this stupid thing."

"Now you can jump it, ride it, and grind it."

"Yeah, but it felt like my board was going to snap in half."

"That's because everything you've ever done on the board was on the wheels."

"True. I want to practise that again."

"Sure."

Jordy looked around as Ali finished the last bit of her cherry slush. He picked out a family across the street that had come down from the suburbs. There were two tells: the kid's running shoes were bright white, and the women were clutching their purses tight to their bodies. *That's right*, Jordy thought, *we're all a bunch of city crooks.*

Ali three-pointed her slush in a trash can and turned to Jordy. "You know, the best place to grind is at the park, because it's all cement."

"That's true."

Ali waited for Jordy to finish his thought, but he didn't. "So let's go to the park."

"Nah."

"Why don't you want to go?" Ali continued. "Is it because of your friends, the ones I saw at the park? You don't ride with them anymore."

Jordy didn't respond.

Ali said matter-of-factly, "So you don't want to go riding with me at the park."

"That's not true. I though you preferred it out here."

She smiled. "Yeah, but if you want to win the competition at the skate part, you have do everything you've learned out here at the skate park."

Ali had been right the first time. Jordy wasn't embarrassed by her. He just couldn't deal with the hazing by Carter and Donavan. He made a decision he knew he might regret. "Let's go to the park. We'll meet up with the boys."

Ali jumped from the bench right onto her board.

They travelled at a snail's pace because of all the foot traffic.

To Jordy's surprise, Ali suggested just what he had been thinking. "Let's take the alleys."

They picked up their boards and dropped them in the first alley they could find. There were still people there, but it wasn't nearly as packed.

Jordy and Ali criss-crossed the entire Market without having to take a main road. They also had a chance to take in some graffiti along the way. To Jordy, graffiti was art, the kind you didn't have to go to some museum to see.

Jordy pointed to the side of a building. "I don't get it. Why would a green alien be riding on a dragon?"

"I think they all tell a story."

"Well then, what does *that* say?"

They slowed down as they neared the back of an

old two-storey building completely covered in art-work. There was blue sky with clouds up near the roof and a rocky mountain rising around the windows. On one side was a white horse with wings, and on the other was a ghoulish knight with a long sword below a bony winged dragon.

Ali took in the image like an expert surveying a painting in a museum. "Looks like a horse with wings staring down a weird dude and his dragon."

Jordan laughed.

"Actually, maybe it's good versus evil."

Jordy nodded. "I bet you're right, but what about that writing? Looks like my dad's Chinese writing."

"Hey, it's all just picture to me."

Jordy turned back to the alley and spotted three figures in the distance. It was Carter, Donavan, and Murph.

Carter whistled and Ali's head swivelled in their direction.

"Hey, there they are," she said.

Jordy let out an unenthusiastic, "Yep."

As the boys approached, they met Ali's smile with dead stares.

Carter, of course, was the first to speak. "Jordy. What a coincidence."

"Actually, we were just coming to find you guys."

Murph looked at Jordy pointedly.

Jordy stammered the introductions. "Oh, this is

Murph, Carter, and Donavan. And this is Ali." He stepped back and waited for the sparks to fly. Instead there was awkward silence.

Murph finally said, "Hi, Ali."

Jordy could tell that Ali sensed the tension, but she didn't let it bother her. "We were just heading to practise for the competition at the park."

"So you ride?" Carter was a master at stating the obvious.

Ali looked down at her skateboard and widened her eyes. "Ah, yes."

Jordy noticed that Carter had a big smile on his face. He didn't like that.

"So, I have a great idea," Carter said, his smile growing wider.

Everyone turned to him.

"Let's race."

"Not today," Jordy said.

Carter said, "We understand if you're not up to it."

Ali innocently sealed the deal by saying, "Okay. Where to?"

Carter smiled. "The skateboard park."

She looked at Jordy as they pushed forward on their boards, but he couldn't meet her eyes. And he could tell that Murph was not happy about Ali by the way he shot ahead into the lead.

Murph started off by jumping a wooden plank that stretched across the alley.

Carter yelled out from behind, "Come on, Murph. You can do better than that."

Jordy followed Murph as he performed a kickflip and then made a sharp turn down another alley. It was so quick that they all had to dodge a couple of angry suburbanites.

Carter grew impatient and stole the lead, smacking Murph on the helmet as he passed him.

Carter spun left and gunned his board down another alley.

Jordy looked back to Ali, who was all smiles. He wanted to impress her by taking the lead, but the alley that Carter entered was a narrow path between two small houses. They had to dodge empty pop cans and beer bottles. and several oversized bags of garbage.

Carter bolted out of the alley and right into Pedestrian Sunday. He cut off the crowd and created a path for everyone to follow him into another alley.

Carter is the reason people hate skateboarders, Jordy thought.

Jordy sped on as graffiti-covered walls passed by at a blurring rate. He saw what looked like a withered tree with blood pouring out of it. *Probably a story about the decaying environment*, Jordy thought. He refocused on the game and looked for an opportunity to take the lead.

He dropped his foot to the ground and pushed as hard as he could past Donavan. Carter was the only one ahead of him now, and he knew eventually the guy would slip up.

Carter led the group down an alley that backed onto homes.

Jordy heard Ali call out his name. He saw the back of a motorcycle starting to back out of a makeshift garage. Instead of warning Carter, Jordy saw it as a chance to take the lead.

Carter hummed along, comfortable as the leader. As the motorcycle engine fired to life and reversed, Carter stumbled off his board.

Jordy jumped ahead into the lead. He decided to take it up a level. He wouldn't make it all about speed and stupidity, he'd throw in some tricks that Carter couldn't resist trying to copy. He ollied over an over-turned plastic garbage can, scraping his back two wheels along it.

Jordy looked back to see everyone manage to ollie over the can. Murph looked at him like he was from Planet X. Just a while ago, he hadn't been able to jump the recycling bin. Jordy sped ahead, but glanced behind to see Ali finally get into the flow of the game by passing Murph.

Carter shouted out, "Make it interesting."

Jordy scanned the alley ahead. He spotted a back-yard with a cement ledge along the alley. He lined it up and launched his board into the air, grinding the base of his deck along the ledge. Jordy looked sideways to see Carter and Donavan ride past him. *Stop trying to impress them*, Jordy thought. *Stick to the race.*

Ali caught up with Jordy as he jumped back into the alley. "Let's go get them."

Jordy called back to Murph, "You in?"

Murph jumped off his board and picked it up. "Actually, I'm out."

Jordy felt torn. This was his chance to make up with Murph, but he really wanted to get Carter back.

He and Ali skateboarded side by side, and they slowly gained ground on the boys. Carter was so sure of himself that he even slowed down so they could catch up.

"What's up with this guy?" Ali asked.

Jordy shrugged his shoulders. "Everything."

Jordy decided to offer Ali some advice. "With this guy, expect the unexpected. He'll even sacrifice Donavan if he has to."

Ali leaped ahead of Jordy and he followed. Carter was turning the game back into a race, and he was hard to catch. He cut across alleys without looking left or right, and even squeezed between two parked cars.

Jordy was in last place, but he was preparing to make his move. He knew Carter would take them back onto the street, and he wanted to stop that.

Ali was in striking distance, but Donavan kept swerving to cut her off. He even swung a few elbows to keep her back. Jordy thought, *I should have known they would play dirty.*

Carter reached a T-junction and made a razor-sharp turn down an alley that led to the busiest part of the Market. Jordy looked down the alley and all he saw were people crossing it.

Carter screamed like a madman and the people crossing the street all looked up in alarm. He made the quick turn onto the sidewalk as people hustled out of the way.

Jordan knew that someone had to end this before it got any worse. On the sidewalk, he watched Ali make her move on Donavan and Carter, who were clearing the way ahead like two snowploughs. He knew she would bring the game back to the alley. She kicked her board into high gear and jumped ahead to pass the boys. Jordy watched helplessly from behind as they tried to sandwich her. She ducked down, and the two boys collided into each other over her head. Ali swerved as Donavan crumpled to the ground. Carter tried to recover but, with only one foot on the board, he lost control and went helmet-first into a sidewalk bin of plastic jewellery. A rainbow of assorted neck-laces and beads exploded into the air.

Jordy caught up with Ali and they examined the crash scene.

Donavan got to his feet and cackled at Carter, who was covered in the cheap jewellery. The two were surrounded by an angry mob who were yelling at them.

Jordy and Ali ducked into the nearest alley and caught their breath.

"So that's Carter." Ali didn't sound impressed.

"Crazy, isn't he?"

"Did we win?"

"Yeah, I think we won."

Jordy held up his hand and Ali high-fived him. Their fingers curled together and locked for a moment before Ali smiled and let go.

8 Is That Your Final Decision?

Jordy picked up his skateboard four stores down from his parent's shop and stopped.

Ali grabbed her board and asked, "Your parents hate that you ride that much, huh?"

"Yeah, they think I'm a menace to society when I'm on this thing."

"My parents actually love that I do it."

"That's because they are cool and probably born in Canada, right?"

"Not really. It's more that they wished everyone would trade in their gas-guzzling cars for bicycles, rollerblades, skateboards, or just plain old walking. Save the environment, and all that."

"I think that makes them cool."

"But they take it to the extreme. Everything has to be biodegradable. Even my jeans are made of hemp."

"Biode — ?"

"Means it can be recycled."

"I thought my parents were weird."

"All parents are wacky to different degrees."

"Mom thinks she is psychic, and when my dad is alone in the store he sings out loud. Really loud."

Ali laughed. "That's okay. My dad coughs every time he farts."

Jordy laughed and stepped out of the way of a customer exiting a cheese shop. He got hit with the smell of a stinky cheese as it escaped from the store. It smelled like a garbage truck filled to the brim with day-old tuna salad.

"That's disgusting."

The customer snarled at him.

Jordy and Ali laughed and started to walk toward home.

"So, do you think your friends liked me?"

"Yes. Why?"

"I think I might have upset Donavan. And especially Carter."

"It's not your fault that you're an amazing skateboarder."

"But that bin he hit …"

Jordy laughed. "Why's it your fault? He tried to cut you off and bumped into Donavan."

"I guess so."

Jordy said goodbye to Ali and entered the produce shop. Two stragglers finished shopping and slowly made their way to the counter to pay for their food.

Jordy's Dad called those kinds of shoppers foot-draggers. As they left, Jordy and his dad followed them outside. He helped his dad drag wooden trays carrying cartons of fruit inside the store. Then Jordy grabbed a long metal pole and stuck it into a groove below their canopy. He wound it counter-clockwise until it was flush with the store's sign as his dad hosed the sidewalk down. Jordy's dad locked the main doors, and then Jordy followed him upstairs for dinner.

On Sunday nights the apartment smelled like heaven. It was the only night of the week that the family ate together, and Mom always made a feast. Jordy washed up and joined everyone at the kitchen table.

Dad said grace and everyone dug in. Jordy grabbed a pair of plastic chopsticks and picked up a piece of fish, at the same time scooping a few vegetables onto his plate. With the store downstairs, the food was always the freshest, the best of the best.

Everyone was quietly eating until Dad spoke. "So, Jordy, what are you going to do this summer?"

Jordy knew it was a trick question.

"We have some suggestions."

He was right!

His mom added, "There's a backyard day camp. Kids play basketball and soccer and there are lots of other activities."

"They even have badminton," said his dad.

Jordy picked at his fish. "No …"

His mom quickly continued, "For you and your brother."

He didn't want to be stuck babysitting his brother at a stupid camp playing badminton for two months. That would be a nightmare. "Last summer Simon stayed in the store."

Jordy's mom passed him a bowl of noodles. He looked at her plate; it was untouched. She had spent four hours preparing a meal that she wasn't eating.

"Yes, but he is older now," she said. "He can only sit around the store for so long."

Jordy looked at his brother, who was watching his summer being organized for him, then back to his mom. "He hates the summer and is happy in the cold room."

He got a double stare from his parents.

His dad said, "You want to do what you want to do, but you also have responsibilities."

Jordy knew he had to go all-or-nothing. "The Community Centre opened a skateboard park. I'm going to be there the whole summer, and it is totally safe. They have some vertical ramps and rails, but they're not dangerous. All I do is ollie them."

His dad tilted his head. "Ollie?"

He looked at his parents, who looked at each other. Had he said too much?

His mom said, "The camp was just one idea," before finally taking a bite of her food.

Jordy nodded, trying to hide his surprise. Maybe they weren't just trying to sabotage his summer. Maybe they just wanted him to involve his little brother in his life.

★ ★ ★

Jordy was walking briskly across the second floor of the school when he spotted the back of Murph's backpack bobbing along in front of him. He caught up with him just as they reached their lockers.

"How's it going?" Jordy asked.

Murph shrugged his shoulders.

"You missed Carter's wipeout. It was ten times more embarrassing than mine."

Murph nodded.

"So, are you worried about final report card coming out on Friday?"

Murph shook his head and turned to poke his head into his locker.

"That was a joke. You're going to get all eighties."

Murph still didn't respond.

"What's up? Do I smell bad?"

Before Murph could decide whether or not to answer, Carter and Donavan had arrived.

Carter poked Jordy with his finger. "That chick is a horrible skateboarder."

"She's better than all of us." Jordy knew Carter

hated being embarrassed. "Carter, you're just angry because she out-rode you and you were left cleaning up that mess."

Donavan and Murph were smart enough to back away.

"At least I'm not abandoning my friends for some girlfriend."

"She's not my girlfriend. She's just a girl ..."

"Okay, then at least I'm not the one deserting my friends for just a girl. A girl who wants you all for herself."

"You don't know what you're talking about."

Carter turned to Donavan and Murph for support. "Am I right, guys?"

Jordy looked at Murph. He didn't look back, keeping his gaze on Carter.

"You are totally wrong," Jordy protested. If only Ali did like him that way!

They all shut up when a teacher walked by. Jordy was glad for the chance to just stop the conversation. Why were they all turning on him?

When the teacher was out of earshot, Carter continued, "You need to make a choice. Ride with us or ride with her. You can't have it both ways."

"What?" Jordy looked at Carter and Donavan. He stared at Murph in disbelief until Murph looked away. *How could Murph side with these two goons?*

Donavan got in Jordy's face, forcing him back up

against a locker. "Yeah, man, make your decision and remember that we're your crew."

Carter leaned in. "So what's it going to be? It shouldn't take you this long to figure out who your friends are."

Donavan stepped back and held his hands out. "He's actually thinking about choosing that girl."

Jordy wanted to reach out and smack Donavan. He blurted out, "Fine. You want my decision. I choose her."

That caught the boys off guard. They couldn't do anything but shut up and walk away. Jordy watched as Murph followed Donavan and Carter. With a split-second decision, he had lost eleven years of friendships.

9 Autopilot

Jordy kicked down on his board and grabbed it when it flipped up. Ali wanted to check out the art show at the small park in the Market.

"I won't be long," she said.

Jordy could barely see the grass for all the artists' tables set out and the potential customers traipsing across it. He stepped off the curb and ventured into the park. He walked up to a statue. It was a bronze man wearing a jacket and turtleneck sweater, standing between two park benches. It was so lifelike, he had to go up to it and wave his hand in front of its face. The statue didn't move.

Ali dragged Jordy off to show him a painting she liked. He didn't get it. It looked like the artist had taken a few cans of paint and just dropped them on the painting. He smiled politely at the artist and thought, *who would ever spend a hundred and fifty dollars on that thing?*

"I'm going to tell Mom about it. She'll love it," Ali said.

Jordy smiled, and thought, *well, that's who.*

Jordy and Ali got back on their boards and headed for the skateboard park.

Ali adjusted her helmet and said, "I can't believe school is over after tomorrow."

"The month really flew by." But, after what happened at school with his friends, Jordy was finding it hard to get excited about summer starting. He was still in shock and unable to sleep properly, but he couldn't let Ali know. Jordy pulled his lower lip over his top lip and looked at Ali on her board. She had no idea that he had chosen her over his friends.

Ali's voice broke into his thoughts. "Are you okay?"

"I'm fine."

"You're nervous about the competition."

That sounded like a reasonable enough excuse. He nodded.

"You'll do great."

Jordy looked up to his left and saw a big hospital looming over the tree line. It made him feel even sicker. He wanted to check in and ask if they had the technology to erase Carter, Donavan, and especially Murph from his memory. One simple brain scan and his best friends could become instant strangers.

"It's busy."

He looked up when he heard Ali's voice. They were standing at the gate to the skateboard park. "Looks busier than the day it opened."

"Now you see why I prefer the streets."

"Want to turn around?" If she said yes, he wouldn't have to risk seeing the guys.

"Competition's on Saturday. Time to skate the park."

As they rolled into the park, Ali offered him some words of encouragement. "Remember that eighty percent of the kids here are amateur wannabes."

Jordy smiled for the first time all day. Her words refocused him. He remembered his goal. He wanted to win the competition and get a new skateboard. The icing on the trophy would be to beat Carter.

Ali said, "Let's do this."

He followed her into a U-shaped vertical ramp. They skateboarded up and down, each time getting higher in the air. It felt good to be back at the park with his eyes on the big prize.

As Jordy got into a nice groove on the ramp, his mind drifted. He imagined himself riding on Saturday and being on his best game. His ollie, grind, and one-eighties were flawless. He pictured the final round. He would start strong by dropping into the bowl and fly out the other end with the board at his feet. The waiting skateboarders would cheer for him, envious that he was the one pushing the envelope. But he wasn't done

86

yet. He knew to seal the deal he'd have to pull a move that no one could predict — not even the judges. He would swoosh back and forth on the vertical ramp, doing kickflips up one side and one-eighties up the other. At this point, half of the Market would have abandoned their stores to watch Jordy. He'd then hush the overcrowded skateboard park by faking the last one-eighty, instead flying off the other end of the vertical ramp into an airborne somersault. The awed silence would be broken by a standing ovation as he landed the trick and came to a stop. The final piece to his dream puzzle was Ali stepping forward from the crowd and giving him a big hug — and an even bigger kiss.

"Jordy."

He flashed back to reality. "Huh?"

"You going to go back and forth all day?"

"No."

He reached the top of one side of the ramp and turned into a one-eighty. When he was 120 degrees into the turn, he lost sight of his board and knew he couldn't land it. Falling fast, he pulled his feet up behind him so he could crash land. He slid to the bottom of the ramp and searched for his board.

Jordy kept his head down so Ali couldn't see his frustration. He grabbed his skateboard and rode it past the series of molehills that he had ridden with Murph a century ago. Then he waited with riders who were lined up for their turn on the lip of the bowl. He was anxious to try dropping in.

By the time Jordy got to the front of the line, he was watching two kids who had no right to be hogging the bowl. They were clearly inexperienced, and Jordy was impressed that they came out the other end alive.

Jordy used his back foot to hold his board down over the drop. But when he placed his front foot on the board, he immediately dropped down. He raced downward, unhappy that he hadn't been able to hold himself up. At the bottom of the bowl, he had to bail. Frustrated, he jumped to his feet and waited for his board to return down the other side of the bowl.

He tried again, thinking that dropping in on the ramp in the parking lot had been much easier because it wasn't as steep. The only thing that would make the parking-garage ramp harder would be a car driving up. But his foot slipped and again he dropped into the bowl out of control. Getting more and more upset with himself, Jordy returned to the top once more.

Ali asked if he was okay.

Jordy nodded, staring at the far end of the park.

"Remember to push down on your back foot," she said.

"Uh-huh." He wasn't listening. He had spotted Carter and Donavan on one of the rails. They were going back and forth, grinding it each way.

"So they *are* upset."

"What?"

She pointed where he was staring. "You're staying away from them."

He tried to stop his mouth from letting words slip out. "Actually, they're staying away from me."

"Because of the race."

Jordy had already said too much.

"Jordy?"

He turned to her. "Because they're dumb enough to think we're a couple."

"What? That's ridiculous."

Jordy looked away. He tried to process what she was saying. *So, I like her, but she doesn't like me.* He chose her over his friends for nothing!

Jordy turned to Ali and said, "I know, that's what I told them. Let's just ride."

He continued to skateboard, but had a hard time focusing. He didn't understand why he couldn't pull off tricks that a day before he had done expertly. He pushed himself until the sun crept below the horizon.

★ ★ ★

At home, Jordy turned on his autopilot and shut down inside. He retrieved his brother from the cold room and briskly escorted him upstairs. Ignoring the TV in the next room, Jordy cut carrots and placed them on top of a salad. He turned on the oven, heated leftovers from Sunday, and stared deep into nowhere.

The oven timer dinged and Jordy barely noticed. Like a well-programmed robot, he took the food out of the oven and placed it on plates. He walked into the family room and turned off the TV.

Simon got the hint and joined his brother at the kitchen table.

"Can I come watch the competition?"

Jordy didn't respond.

"It's on Saturday, right?"

Jordy deflected each of his brother's questions with the frown that seemed stuck firmly to his face.

"Can you believe that tomorrow's the last day of school?"

Jordy gobbled down his food.

"I'm so happy."

Jordy put his fork down and waited silently for Simon to finish his food.

"Is there dessert?"

Jordy shook his head and took the plates to the sink. He washed and dried them, and then turned the TV back on for Simon. He went to his room and closed the door.

Jordy stared down at his battered skateboard. His friends said that he had abandoned them, but it was really the other way around. *Skateboarding is a lonely sport,* Jordy thought. *It doesn't matter if you have friends or not. The only person you're playing against is you.* What he needed to do was block them out and push himself more. If he let them get to him, the distractions would continue to bring him down.

He dropped the board on its wheels and jumped off his bed onto it. He stood and bounced up and down. Either way, this tournament would be the board's last run. So he might as well push it to the brink and walk away with a new one. The old board would make great firewood.

There was a light knock on the bedroom door. It was his mom, tapping on the door to the tune of her favourite Chinese nursery rhyme. Like his board, it was way past retirement.

"Yeah," he said, just loud enough to be heard through the door.

His mom poked her head in. After a long day at the store, her voice was very quiet. "Simon said you were upset."

Jordy slid his skateboard under his bed. "Just a little stressed."

She entered, closed the door, and leaned against it. "Tomorrow's the last day of school. What is there to be stressed about?"

"It's not that."

She tilted her head and looked at Jordy. "Is it about skateboarding?"

Jordy couldn't believe it. *She is psychic!* "How did you know?"

"With you, honey, it's either school or skateboarding."

"Or Simon."

"Yes."

"There's a skateboarding competition this weekend."

"Why didn't you tell us?"

"Why would I? You guys hate skateboarding."

"Hate's a strong word. Dislike."

"I really want to win."

"It's just a game." His mother let out a lion-size yawn. "But I'd still like to see you compete. Maybe it would help me understand why you like it so much."

"Yeah, but Dad won't close the store."

"You're right. The weekend's our busiest time. Can you change the time of the competition?"

Jordy shook his head and smiled.

"We'll figure something out. Try to get some sleep. And please be nice to your brother. He loves you."

"I know."

His mom closed the door behind her and Jordy dug his skateboard out from under his bed. He jumped on it. He didn't want his goal to slip away. He knew the only way to do that was to cut off his emotions. They were getting in the way.

10 Abandoned

Jordy's right and left brain battled it out as he tried to calculate a math problem while keeping his balance on his skateboard. *If there are ten months in the school year and five days in a week*, he thought, *how many trips do I make to school?* It wasn't easy. He jerked his right hand out to stop himself from falling over. He knew there were about two hundred days of school, but having to subtract all the holidays made it really difficult.

Jordy was really just trying to distract himself from the reality that he was skateboarding to school alone. He should have been with his friends, celebrating the last day of school and making plans for the summer. Instead, he didn't even have Murph to talk to, and he was probably facing a whole summer of badminton at a day camp with his little brother. He had made it halfway to school before his feelings began to creep under his skin. He pushed them away by lifting the front of his skateboard up into a manual. The feelings continued, so he kickflipped his board into the air and landed it. He knew that if he could keep his feelings at bay, he would be okay.

On the bright side, he had come a long way since meeting Ali. She had helped him in ways that his friends couldn't. They were all about competing. They wouldn't want to give away their trade secrets.

★ ★ ★

"Okay everyone," Mr. Fletcher said. "Can we clean up with a little less noise?"

Jordy looked up from the floor in his classroom. The room looked like a landfill dump and they had only two periods to clean it up. Desks were jammed against the sides of the room and chairs were piled on top of each other, practically pushing through the ceiling. Everyone had monster-size piles of papers and files on the floor. Jordy looked back down at his. He rifled through his English and History folders. He saw a collection of short stories and a few newspaper articles he had written. Both had received respectable B-minuses. He pulled out a thick poetry assignment. Beside his name, at the bottom of the title page, was Murph's. The assignment was Jordy's one and only A-minus grade, and that was completely due to Murph's hard work. Jordy tore it in two and three-pointed it into the recycling bin. He did the same to a stack of grammar worksheets, as if he was never going to attend school again.

Mr. Fletcher was trying to squeeze every last drop out of the year. "Jordan, please come to the front. Please distribute these."

Jordy took the papers and wondered why he had to be the one to track down every classmate and hand them back. He read the first name on top of the pile: Carter. He trashed the paper and began to search for the other students, who were scattered all over the room. After recycling Donavan's paper, he held Murph's paper in his hand.

Jordy knew he couldn't just toss Murph's paper. Murph kept a mental inventory of everything. He would investigate the disappearance of any stray assignment. Even if it was after school had let out for the summer, he would show up to try and find Mr. Fletcher. If he couldn't find the teacher in the summer, then he'd do it the first day back in September.

Jordy put Murph's paper into the classroom's lost-and-found box. It would be the first place his friend — his ex-friend — would look.

Jordy thought the day would never end. His teacher gave the "have a safe summer" speech, and then the class did the big countdown. Watching the clock above the door as the last thirty seconds slipped away was more of an event than the countdowns for New Years and the space shuttle launch combined.

Within the first three seconds of freedom, Jordy's

mind shifted to the skateboarding competition.

★ ★ ★

The chicken was so dry, it took a big chug of juice to get it down. Jordy took what was left on his plate and tossed it. He watched his brother chew on his own leathery piece.

Simon spoke around the half-gnawed chicken in his mouth. "Want to watch TV after?"

"Actually, I'm going out."

"Where?"

"The parking garage."

"What? Why?"

"None of your business."

The second that Simon's chicken touched the plate, Jordy snatched it up and emptied it into the garbage.

"I was still eating that," Simon complained.

"You weren't eating it; you were sharpening your teeth." Jordy tucked his chair under the table and said, "Let's go." He triple-checked that the stove was off before heading downstairs.

The store wasn't busy. His mom was dusting the azaleas and his dad drizzled water on lettuce heads to keep them fresh.

His mom asked, "How was dinner?"

"Great, Mom. Can I go out now?"

Jordy's dad flicked at a fruitfly circling a bushel of carrots and was about to say no.

"I told him it was okay," his mom said.

Jordy knew that his dad knew better than to argue with her. But he still had to have the last word, as if to prove that he was really in charge.

"Fine, but take your brother."

Jordy opened his mouth, but nothing came out. He couldn't fight that one.

"And be back in an hour."

Jordy had his skateboard in one hand and his brother's arm in the other. They crossed the street and entered the parking garage. The top three floors were vacant. He sat his brother down beside the door to the stairs and jumped on his board.

"Don't move."

Simon nodded his head.

"But if you see someone, run."

Simon nodded his head again.

Jordy approached the long line of cement blocks that kept the building from toppling over. He set his board into motion and wove around each one. With every slalom, he felt his game return. He looped around the last one and headed back even faster. He whooshed past his brother, who was watching his every move with eyes wide and pupils dilated.

Jordy spotted a mound of rubble and hurried toward it. He could hear Ali's advice as he ollied up and over it. This was the place where he first learned to pull off pro tricks. The top floors of the garage were magical — the perfect place to practise for the competition.

Jordy was concentrating so hard that he was surprised to see that Simon had caught up with him and was running by his side.

"Did you see someone?" he asked his little brother.

"No."

Jordy smiled and came to a stop at the edge of the ramp going down to the next floor.

Simon panted as he pulled up next to Jordy and stared at his brother. "Where are you going now?"

Jordy pointed. "Down." He positioned his skateboard on the lip of the ramp as his brother stood perched on it. "Three, two, one ..." Jordy lowered his board. His speed went from zero to sixty in no time. The wheels and trucks under his board rattled as he looked back to his brother barrelling toward him. As he hit the bottom, he spotted Ali in a blur. She was climbing the stairs toward the top floor.

"Ali!"

She didn't hear him, so he did a large arcing turn and passed his brother as he headed back toward the ramp.

"Where are you going?"

"Back up!"

Jordy kept his speed up as he hit the ramp. Almost

immediately, he began to lose speed, and halfway up he hopped off his board just before it started sliding back down. He ran the rest of the way up, emerging at the top of the ramp just as Ali came through a green door.

He greeted her with a big smile.

"Who's that?"

Jordy was surprised to see Simon appear over the crest of the ramp. He was bent over and gasping for air, but he was still moving fast.

"My brother."

"Oh." She unhinged her skateboard helmet.

"I was just practising for tomorrow."

"Hey, I bumped into Murph on the street yesterday."

Her comment came out of nowhere, "Really."

"Yep." She brushed a strand of runaway hair that swung over her eyes. "We talked. He told me what happened."

Jordy looked at his brother, who was leaning against a post. He wished the little guy would disappear.

"I figured something was up, but I didn't know you guys stopped hanging out," Ali continued.

"It's just a little squabble. We've had them before, and we always get over it." Why was he lying to her?

"The way he put it, it seemed a lot bigger. More serious."

"I told you, he thinks you and I are going out. He's probably jealous."

"Actually, he said that you just stopped hanging out with him."

Jordy didn't know what to say. Why was this coming up now? All he wanted to do was focus on tomorrow.

Ali's voice cracked when she spoke. "I don't want to come between friends."

"You're not."

"I am."

"How long have you known Murph?"

"I don't know … eleven years."

"That's a long time. If it was me, I wouldn't want to be treated that way."

For the first time since he bumped into her at the skate park, Jordy didn't have a thing to say to Ali. A cold lump materialized in his throat. "Uh-huh."

She looked at Simon and then whispered to Jordy, "God. Why do I feel like we're breaking up? This is stupid."

Her words hurt. He realized that, deep down, he liked her and nothing she said could change how he felt inside.

Jordy knew Ali's mission was complete when she got back on her board. He nodded his head as if to say, it was okay if she needed to go.

She did.

11 Meltdown

Jordy sat squished on a long bench with his skateboard pressed against his knees. He peered left and then right. There were skateboarders as far as his eyes could see.

To stand a chance at doing well in this competition, he would have to get in the zone. He tried to push back everything that had happened in the last few weeks, especially his meeting with Ali in the parking garage. *Concentrate on the competition.* He tugged at the white mesh vest he wore over his black T-shirt. It had *Kumani's Sports Store* on it in big bold letters, and below that was the number 68. He felt like he really was just a number.

Jordy looked out at the skate park. Mr. Kumani's name was everywhere. It was an advertising blitz for the small sports store — the Kumani's banners flapping in the wind were bigger than the Community Centre's Canadian flag. A young skateboarding hopeful caught

Jordy's attention as he whizzed by the long bench. The kid turned onto a ramp and tried to do a three-sixty when he went airborne. Jordy cringed as the kid wiped out hard.

A couple of community workers ran out to the downed kid. They were first on the scene and watched over him as a EMS crew appeared and jumped into action. They taped the kid to a stretcher and wheeled him off.

Not a great way to start a competition — and an even worse way to advertise, Jordy thought. *Come to Kumani's Sports Store, pick out a board from our wide selection. That's Kumani's Sports Store. Hope you don't crack an ankle!* Jordy shook his head. He was definitely in a bad mood.

Jordy spotted Mr. Blight resetting his giant stop-watch before stepping up to the microphone. "Up next, number fifty-four," blared the loudspeaker.

Murph stood up and hopped on his board. Jordy just couldn't watch, so he stood up and walked passed the row of benches.

A community worker stopped him. "Can I help you?"

"I have to pee."

He let Jordy go.

Jordy looked out at the crowd. Behind him were stands weighted down by families watching the action. Behind the stands, a local restaurant had set up a booth selling wrap sandwiches. Competing with them was an old-looking man and his hot dog stand. Tourists strolled the area as a few artists, including the one Ali had been talking to last week, set up their work. Jordy passed a row of porta-potties and returned to his spot on the bench.

Murph had completed his run and another skater was taking centre stage. Jordy hated the way they were randomly calling numbers. You had to always be ready, adrenaline pumping, because you never knew when it was your turn.

Two riders later, Jordy thought he heard his number called. He looked down at his vest and saw 89. It took him a second to realize that he was looking at it upside down and backwards. They were calling number 68 — his number!

Jordy stood up, got on his board, and rode to his starting position at the highest point of the cement bowl. He pushed down on the tail of his skateboard. His back wheels wedged against the cement lip and his front wheels hung over the drop. Then he looked up. Bad idea. He immediately flushed as he felt the heat of the stares of a crowd full of strangers. It was just a sea of eyeballs.

He lost his balance and his board started to drop. He whipped his front foot onto it and just held on. He had been planning to do a fancy drop-in, followed by a tailgrab coming out the other end. All he could think now was how weird it was that all his practising came down to a four-minute ride. Out of control, he hit the bottom of the bowl and had a déjà-vu moment — he felt like he was being flushed down a toilet bowl.

His stomach dropped as he popped up the other end. He dragged his heel to slow down so he wouldn't crash. Somehow, he survived and made it to solid ground.

Nothing to do but go on. He sped up and aligned himself along a square rail to prepare for his next trick. Just before reaching the rail, he popped his head up and pushed down on the board. He went airborne, landed on the rail, and glided along it. He wasn't thinking about the exhilaration of vying for the number-one spot. The only thing in his brain were Ali's words — *keep your head up*. It felt strange to be performing her tricks.

He jumped off the rail and tried to stay in the zone. He directed his board toward a series of hills. He sped into the first series of bumps and grooved through them, bobbing up and down. He did his best to carve into each one, but he found his mind drifting again. It felt like just yesterday that he was doing the mini hills with Murph at his side. His feelings were seeping through like water leaking through a dam. How could things have gone so wrong so quickly? He didn't have answers, and this wasn't the time or place to figure it out.

Cool it, Jordy thought. *Get yourself together.* He bought some time to quiet his thoughts by speeding along the perimeter of the park. He was off his game and he didn't know how to get it back. Passing by the row of skateboarders, he spotted Carter and Donavan. They were the only ones laughing.

Jordy swerved back into the action and tried to make the most of the minute he had left. He wasn't pulling off his best tricks, so he rode up the closest platform and performed the trick he mastered in his bedroom. With time running down, he did three kick-flips in a row. Jordy decided to stick to the tricks he had practised on the old shag rug in his room. He did a wheelie, lifting the front of his board as he travelled up a shallow ramp. He levelled it out and transitioned down the ramp, and did a reverse manual, lifting his back wheels up in the air. It wasn't his best, but it was all he could bring. He rode the backward wheelie as the red numbers on the digital clock counted down the last seconds of his ride.

Jordy grabbed his board and sat down on the bench. His four minutes had seemed to last forever, but he had barely broken a sweat. He was disappointed that he couldn't concentrate. He couldn't stop the flood of bottled-up emotions. Why was he even in the competition? He was going to be alone all summer, and beating his friends wasn't going to change that. He wished he could just push his reset button. He needed to reboot, realign, refocus, or quit. The only bright spot was that he hadn't fallen.

Jordy's ordeal wasn't over. Carter, Donavan, and Ali still had to ride. Carter was up. He wowed the judges as he ollied up onto a high platform and then did a frontside flip off the other end. Carter picked up speed and trekked backward up a ramp. When he turned around at the top, his front wheels caught the lip and he fell off his board.

Jordy hated the thought that he was relying on others to fall and fail so he could make it in the top twenty.

Carter got back up. The rest of his four minutes was filled with the kind of riding Jordy wished he had done. In his typical style, Carter rolled by the judges and took a moving bow, as if he had just performed the greatest opera ever.

Next up was Donavan, who wowed the crowd by outriding Carter. Donavan pulled off a big nosegrind, did an awesome frontside flip, and landed a high-flying jump out of the bowl. Two riders later, Ali stood up and began by ollying a rail and doing a stellar nosegrind, grinding the rail with the front truck of her skateboard.

Again, Jordy just couldn't watch. He excused himself down the bench, and was stopped by the same community worker.

The community worker acted like he was in charge of the universe. "Let me guess, you have to pee again?"

Jordy nodded. He took a seat on the ground across from the artists, where tourists were still blowing their hard-earned cash on the primitive paintings. Still, out of everyone there, the busiest person was the hot dog vendor.

Jordy rode out the rest of the day's competition people watching. The only reason he stuck around was to see just how poorly he placed — and to return his vest. The end of the first day of competition was signalled by people pouring out of the stands.

The bullhorn announced that the top-twenty list would be posted in a half hour by the gates. The area surrounding the skate park was so overcrowded that Jordy couldn't see anything. It reminded him of Exhibition Stadium in August; all it was missing was the CNE's candyfloss, three-ring toss, and ancient roller coasters.

He stood up and wandered toward the gates. The quicker he saw the results the quicker he could leave. The list was swarmed by tons of skateboarders. Everyone was pushing and elbowing their way to the front, and Jordy found himself in the middle of the pack. From the corner of his eye, he noticed Carter grinning at him. Jordy tried to ignore him as he scanned the list: Ali was near the top, in the middle were Carter and Donavan. Jordy began to sweat as he continued looking down. He was sort of glad to see Murph was fifth from the bottom. In the very last spot Jordy spotted his name. The way he had ridden, he should have been jumping up and down to have made the top twenty. Instead, he felt angry that blind luck got him through to the second day of competition. He knew that he couldn't win by playing it safe. The big question was, did he want to show up at all?

Jordy cut across a few darkened alleys to keep his distance from the crowd. He didn't have the heart to ride; he walked home with his skateboard in his hand. He popped out of an alley and entered the family store, to find his dad sitting on a counter, reading the local Chinese newspaper.

"You're late," he said, without taking his eyes from his newspaper.

"I was out."

"I know you were out." He turned the page and continued to read. "You have responsibilities here. Your mother and brother depend on you." His dad's voice was quiet.

"What do you want from me?" asked Jordan. *Not now*, he thought, *not today*.

His dad closed the paper, folded it neatly, and rested it on the counter.

"You were skateboarding."

"Mom told you."

"I'm not blind."

The hairs on Jordy's back and arms stood up. He wasn't in the mood for this. "Well don't worry about me skateboarding anymore. Today was my last day. I'm done."

His dad's eyes widened.

Jordy started moving toward the door that led to upstairs.

His dad touched his arm to stop him. "Wait."

Jordy looked his dad in the eyes. "I can't do this right now. I just want to go upstairs." He really didn't want to cry in front of his dad.

"No. We need to talk now."

"No!"

"Please."

Jordy didn't move. His emotions were on overdrive and he felt like he had a fireball inside him. He couldn't control his mouth as words emptied out. "Everything's changed. I haven't seen Murph in forever. Or any of my other friends. Actually, I have no more friends. They won't talk to me, thanks to this skateboarding competition."

Jordy's arms flapped up and down as he talked. If a passerby looked through the store window, they would probably think he was trying to fly.

"What happened between you and Murphy?"

Jordy wiped away a few premature tears with the back of his hand. "I deserted Murphy. He thought I liked Ali. I did, but I didn't know. Carter and Murph don't care.

Dad nodded his head before saying, "Who is Ali?"

"A girl who skateboards … a girl I like. But she won't talk to me either, anymore."

"Oh."

On the one hand Jordy felt good to finally get it all out. But it felt weird to finally admit out loud that he liked Ali.

His dad rubbed his fingers against his cheek. "It seems to me that you have been so focused on this skateboarding competition that you've lost sight of the people who are really important in your life."

Jordy smiled. That was the most his dad had said to him in years.

"Think about the people that you have known for a long time. Friendships."

Jordy nodded.

"But for now, I think you need to sleep." His dad locked the front door of the store and flipped the Open sign so it was facing inside. He was about to shut off the lights. "I was talking with your mother, and, well, I promise to stop pushing the day camp."

"Thanks."

"It was just that I used to play badminton."

"I understand." Jordy had seen one black-and-white picture of his dad playing.

"Will you think about soccer?" his dad asked with a smile.

Jordy smiled back, exhausted. "No."

12 Riding High

For Jordy, waking up Sunday was like coming out of a coma. His eyes were crusted with the left-over tears that had dried up during his deep sleep. When he lifted his head from the pillow, it took him a few seconds to realize that it was summer, there was no school, and it was Sunday. His eyes focused on the alarm clock beside his bed. And the skateboarding competition started in a half hour. He slipped on jeans and a T-shirt at the same time, skipped the brushing of the teeth, and barrelled out of his room.

The apartment was empty. He grabbed his skateboard, which he found upside down on the kitchen table. There was a note next to it: *Good luck.* was all it said.

Jordy shot down the stairs and outside into the sunshine. The fastest way to the park would be by skateboard through the back alleyways. It was a bumpy ride, but at least he didn't have to deal with the weekend crowds on the street.

The skate park was even busier than it had been the day before. And today there were only twenty people competing. Jordy registered, put on his vest, and entered the gates to the park. The first contestant was already out skateboarding. Everyone's eyes were on the competitor as Jordy walked along the long bench to his seat.

He stopped in front of Murph, Carter, and Donavan.

Carter stood up. "Hey, it's Last-Place Jordy."

Jordy tried to look past him at Murph. "Hey, Murph."

Carter blocked his way. "He's not interested. Go away."

Jordy talked over Carter to his best friend. "Murph, I'm sorry for bailing on you. I didn't mean to."

Carter pushed Jordy away, but Jordy just stepped forward again.

"Come on, Murph, I'm giving you a public apology. I was an idiot."

Murph stood up and batted Carter out of the way. "You are an idiot," he said to Jordy, "... for not apologizing earlier." He high-fived his best friend. "It's about time."

"You can have him," Carter shouted to no one in particular. "He's a weasel."

Murph turned to face Carter. He looked past him to Donavan. "Hey, D, want to come with us?"

To Jordy's surprise, Donavan didn't say anything. He was actually considering it.

Carter jumped in. "Donavan's not going anywhere."

"Well, think about it," Murph said, still ignoring Carter. "You know where we are."

Jordy followed Murph to another spot on the bench. "You were amazing."

Murph shrugged his shoulders. "I guess hanging out with Carter toughened me up."

They sat and watched the first five competitors ride. Jordy knew he would have to be the one to get the ball rolling.

"So you spoke to Ali"

"Yeah, I saw her on the street."

Jordy chose his words carefully. "She was really upset."

"She felt like she ruined all your friendships."

"That was Carter ..."

"I tried to tell her that. Jordy, I think Ali just felt that you were going through stuff, and she wanted to give you time to get everything straight. You know, when the competition was over."

Jordy nodded his head slowly. "Smart girl."

There was a moment of silence. It was broken by Murph. "She likes you."

"No, she doesn't."

"Actually she does. She told me."

Jordy looked across the row of seats past Carter and Donavan. Ali was on her feet, getting ready to go next.

Ali started with a big one-eighty off a ramp. She landed it and rolled up another ramp facing backward. She landed, flipped her feet so she was facing forward, and flew into the giant bowl. She went up and down, criss-crossing like a funky pendulum. As she reached the top of each lip, she grabbed the back of her skateboard, and let go before turning back down.

She was a pro out there. Jordy felt lucky that he even knew her. Her last move guaranteed her a top-three spot: She got enough height in the bowl to stop on the ledge; then she dropped in and disappeared inside the bowl. Jordy watched her as she popped out the other end and landed gracefully. Ali ended her run by wowing the judges and crowd with a railstand. She flipped her skateboard on its side and stood on the thin edge. She smiled as her pink wheels and trucks were exposed to the audience.

Jordy heard the judge call his name. He got to his feet and looked to Murph for advice.

"Just go for it." Murph had three seconds to build Jordy's confidence. "You've got nothing to lose."

Jordy tightened his helmet and got on his board. "Thanks."

He pushed his left foot against the ground and began to roll out.

"Jordy."

He turned to look back at Murph.

"Just imagine you're skateboarding the alleys."

Jordy smiled and turned back to focus on his ride. He set himself on top of the giant cement bowl. Looking down, he placed his skateboard into position for a drop in before vertigo kicked in.

Jordy took a deep breath. He stood on his board, defying gravity. He looked out at the crowd, enjoyed the moment, and then slammed his front foot down on the front tip of his board. He plunged below the horizon, picking up speed as he rocketed toward the belly of the bowl. Jordy hit the bottom and his stomach jerked up — he was already accelerating skyward. His thoughts were blurred as he tried to figure out how he would, or even if he would, land. *Out on the streets you have to be flexible and go with the flow*, he thought.

As he approached the edge of the bowl, he made a sharp right turn. That caught everyone off guard, including himself. He found himself in a spiral spin around the inside of the bowl. He kept his elbows up and out to adjust his balance. As his speed slowed, he kept just enough momentum to turn and make it up the wall. Jordy escaped the bowl and landed softly on level land.

He looked up and noticed that the crowd was standing so they could peer inside the bowl.

The old wheels of Jordy's skateboard wobbled as

he kicked it into high gear. He aligned himself with the rail and adjusted his speed so it was just right. As he approached, he kicked the back of his skateboard into an ollie and aimed his trucks over the rail's edge. He touched down and grinded his trucks on the rail by pushing down with his knees.

He was running out of rail. Jordy lifted his front trucks up and did a mini ollie to get his board up in the air and then onto the ground.

Jordy turned so he was facing the nearest vertical ramp. He rode up it and then turned back down. At the bottom, he did the one trick he could do in his sleep, because he had practised it over and over in his bedroom: the kickflip. He surprised everyone by doing four in a row.

Back on his wheels, Jordy did a manual toward the molehills. He lowered his board, flipped his feet around so his back foot was in front, and travelled fakie along them.

Jordy felt comfortable on his board again. He was in his zone and he wasn't sticking to anything he planned. He pushed away everything he had learned and just rode his skateboard by feel.

His four minutes were almost up. He had time for one more quick trick.

Jordy swerved full speed past the row of skateboarders and did a heel drag until he came to a stop in the middle of the track. He stood directly in line with Ali. He watched the timer as it counted down from ten seconds.

He flipped his skateboard on its side and landed on its thin edge. He looked up at Ali and smiled. She smiled back. Looking past her and up into the stands, Jordy was so surprised he almost lost his balance. His mom, dad, and brother were in the stands, cheering him on.

Jordy waved up at them in disbelief. He picked up his board and returned to his spot next to Murph. "You'll never believe it. My parents are here."

"You're right, I don't believe you."

"If Mom, Dad, and Simon are here … it means they closed the store."

"That's a first."

"They've kept it open during thunderstorms, when the rain was so heavy it flooded the sidewalks."

"I remember that they were the only store open when that snowstorm shut down the city."

Jordy laughed. "They even kept it open when there was a car crash in front of the store."

Murph laughed.

Jordy and Murph almost missed the announcer calling Murphy's name.

"That's you."

"Oh." Murph stood up and got on his skateboard.

"Remember, Murph, just go for it like you're out on the street."

Murph smirked at him, and headed out.

Jordy stood up to exit the competition area. The same community worker was blocking his way out. "Let me guess, you have to …"

"No." Jordy smiled. "My family's here."

Jordy walked around the man to the entrance of the stands. He yelled up to his parents, "What are you doing here?"

His dad waved and said, "You're mother talked me into it!"

Jordy returned to his seat just as Murph ended his routine. He was the last competitor to skate.

The judge in the yellow golf shirt stood up and thanked everyone who participated. He said he would announce the winners after he had a chance to add up the scores.

People from the stands descended onto the skate park. Jordy's mom gave him a big hug.

"You did really well," his dad said.

"Thanks. The only problem is that I did really badly yesterday. That'll affect my score when he adds them up." Jordy couldn't keep the smile off his face, and hardly remembered how disappointed he had been the day before.

His mom smiled, "But you had fun."

"Of course."

The announcer walked onto the skate park with the final scores. "It was a really close competition. In first place, and the winner of a one-hundred-and-fifty–dollar gift certificate to Kumani's Sports Store, is…"

Jordy looked toward Ali. It had to be her.

"Ali Gomez."

Ali bounced to her feet. She took the gift certificate from the judge and stood next to him.

In second place, and the winner of a hundred-dollar gift certificate to Kumani's Sports Store is …"

Jordy laughed at the obvious advertising plug. *Everyone gets the message*, he thought.

"Donavan Carlton."

Jordy watched Donavan take his spot next to Ali. Carter was blistering mad, but Donavan was all smiles.

Jordy felt a hand on his shoulder. It was his mom's. She said, "It doesn't matter whether you win or not."

"I know."

The last winner was about to be announced. Jordy knew he didn't need to win, but it would be nice to put Carter in his place.

"And in third spot, and the winner of a fifty-dollar gift certificate to Kumani's Sports Store is Jordan …"

Jordy could see Carter about to explode

"… Lee."

It took Jordy a second to process the news. He was truly surprised. His whole family was hugging him, and Murph snuck in to give him a high-ten.

Like a sleepwalker, Jordy walked toward Ali, Donavan, and the judge to pick up his prize.

★ ★ ★

When he got back to his parents, gift certificate in hand, Jordy's thought he heard his dad say that he was going to take Jordy and his friends out for lunch. That couldn't be right, could it?

"Mom, is Dad okay?" Jordy asked.

"I think time away from the store has been good for him."

Jordy approached Murph. "So, you want to go for lunch?"

"Sure. My parents have to pick up my grandmother from the bus station."

"You'll never believe this, but Dad is buying."

"Today is a big day of firsts!" Murph leaned in closer to Jordy. "You should ask Ali."

"Now?"

"If not now, when?"

Jordy approached Ali, who was talking with her parents.

"Congratulations, Ali."

"To you too. I'm surprised you made top three with your old board," she said, grinning.

Jordy smiled. "Yeah, I guess it was never about the board."

She introduced him to her parents. Jordy was a little embarrassed, but he had to ask. "Do you want to go for lunch? My dad is buying."

"For all of us?"

"Yep."

When Ali raised her eyebrows in her parents' direction, they nodded yes.

"Sure."

Jordy and Ali joined everyone gathered around the take-out window of a local pizza restaurant.

Murph took a big bite of his pizza. "This isn't exactly going out for lunch."

"This is as fancy as it gets for Dad."

Ali laughed. "No one's complaining."

Jordy flagged down his parents. "Thank you for coming."

"You did really well today," his dad said.

His mom smiled. "We are proud of you."

"Really?"

Jordy's dad rested his hand on Jordy's shoulder. "I guess we saw a different side of skateboarding ... no sidewalks and cutting people off."

"Dad, that was never me. Why don't you believe me?"

His mom said, "We do believe you, and we know you wouldn't do anything like that. We just started to worry when you started riding in the streets. And then with Carter ..."

"I want to introduce you to someone." He took them to Ali.

Jordy's dad extended his hand. "So this is the girl

who likes dragon fruit."

Ali smiled and shook his hand. "That's me."

"How did you know?" Jordy asked his father.

His mom leaned in toward Ali. "Our son thinks we are old and out to lunch! It's nice to finally meet you."

Jordy turned to his dad and said, "Thanks for lunch. Thanks for everything."

"You're welcome. And, by the way, this is the best pizza in town." Jordy's dad pointed to Murph's slice. "Those are my tomatoes!"

Everyone laughed.

Jordy looked at the group, his friends and family all together. He noticed that his brother was eating pizza with one hand and holding Jordy's skateboard with the other.

★ ★ ★

Jordy stood outside his parent's store. He wondered if he had only dreamed that they actually closed it on a Sunday to watch him compete on his skateboard. On Pedestrian Sunday in Kensington Market everything was busy. The produce store was more than busy, it was crazy.

Jordy adjusted his outgrown elbow pads on Simon's arms, and tapped his brother on the helmet covered in stickers. "How does that feel?"

"Great," Simon said.

Jordy had spent most of his prize on a used skate-board for Simon. With what was left over, he got new pads for himself, and a fresh new helmet that he could plaster with whatever would come next in his life.

"The most important thing to remember is that you have to keep your head up."

Simon stood on the board. It wobbled like a bowl of jelly, but the kid kept his head up. "You mean like this?"

"Perfect. Now try it again."

Jordy jumped on his old skateboard and followed his brother along the sidewalk. He knew he could have used the prize money on upgrading his own board. But he had finally figured it out — it wasn't the board that counted, it was the skater.

Other books you'll enjoy in the
Sports Stories series

Track and Field

❑ *Mikayla's Victory* by Cynthia Bates
Mikayla must compete against her friend if she wants to represent her school at an important track event.

❑ *Fast Finish* by Bill Swan
Noah is fast, so fast he can outrun anyone he knows, even the two tough kids who wait for him every day after school.

❑ *Walker's Runners* by Robert Rayner
Toby Morton hates gym. In fact, he doesn't run for anything — except the classroom door. Then Mr. Walker arrives and persuades Toby to join the running team.

❑ *Mud Run* by Bill Swan
No one in the S.T. Lovey Cross-Country Club is running with the pack, until the new coach demonstrates the value of teamwork.

❑ *Off Track* by Bill Swan
Twelve-year-old Tyler is stuck in summer school and banned from watching TV and playing computer games. His only diversion is training for a triathlon race … except when it comes to the swimming requirement.

Soccer

❑ *Lizzie's Soccer Showdown* by John Danakas
When Lizzie asks why the boys and girls can't play together, she finds herself the new captain of the soccer team.

❑ *Alecia's Challenge* by Sandra Diersch
Thirteen-year-old Alecia has to cope with a new school, a new stepfather, and friends who have suddenly discovered the opposite sex.

❑ *Shut-Out!* by Camilla Reghelini Rivers
David wants to play soccer more than anything, but will the new coach let him?

❑ *Offside!* by Sandra Diersch
Alecia has to confront a new girl who drives her teammates crazy.

❑ *Heads Up!* by Dawn Hunter and Karen Hunter
Do the Warriors really need a new, hot-shot player who skips practice?

❑ *Off the Wall* by Camilla Reghelini Rivers
Lizzie loves indoor soccer, and she's thrilled when her little sister gets into the sport. But when their teams are pitted against each other, Lizzie can only warn her sister to watch out.

❑ *Trapped!* by Michele Martin Bossley
There's a thief on Jane's soccer team, and everyone thinks it's her best friend, Ashley. Jane must find the true culprit to save both Ashley and the team's morale.

❑ *Soccer Star!* by Jacqueline Guest
Samantha longs to show up Carly, the school's reigning soccer star, but her new interest in theatre is taking up a lot of her time. Can she really do it all?

❑ *Miss Little's Losers* by Robert Rayner
The Brunswick Valley School soccer team haven't won a game all season long. When their coach resigns, the only person who will coach them is Miss Little … their former kindergarten teacher!

❑ *Corner Kick* by Bill Swan
A fierce rivalry erupts between Michael Strike, captain of both the school soccer and chess teams, and Zahir, a talented newcomer from the Middle East.

❑ *Just for Kicks* by Robert Rayner
When their parents begin taking their games too seriously, it's up to the soccer-mad gang from Brunswick Valley School to reclaim the spirit of their sport.

❏ *Play On* by Sandra Diersch

Alecia's soccer team is preparing for the championship game but their game is suffering as the players get distracted by other interests. Can they renew their commitment to their sport in order to make it to the finals?

❏ *Suspended* by Robert Rayner

The Brunswick Valley soccer form their own unofficial team after falling foul to the Principal's Code of Conduct. But will they be allowed to play in the championship game before they get discovered?

❏ *Foul Play* by Beverly Scudamore

Remy and Alison play on rival soccer teams. When Remy finds out Alison has a special plan to beat Remy's team in the tournament, she becomes convinced that Alison will sabotage her team's players.

Basketball

❏ *Fast Break* by Michael Coldwell

Moving from Toronto to small-town Nova Scotia was rough, but when Jeff makes the school basketball team he thinks things are looking up.

❏ *Camp All-Star* by Michael Coldwell

In this insider's view of a basketball camp, Jeff Lang encounters some unexpected challenges.

❏ *Nothing but Net* by Michael Coldwell

The Cape Breton Grizzly Bears prepare for an out-of-town basketball tournament they're sure to lose.

❏ *Slam Dunk* by Steven Barwin and Gabriel David Tick

In this sequel to *Roller Hockey Blues*, Mason Ashbury's basketball team adjusts to the arrival of some new players: girls.

❏ *Courage on the Line* by Cynthia Bates

After Amelie changes schools, she must confront difficult former teammates in an extramural match.

❏ *Free Throw* by Jacqueline Guest
Matthew Eagletail must adjust to a new school, a new team and a new father along with five pesky sisters.

❏ *Triple Threat* by Jacqueline Guest
Matthew's cyber-pal Free Throw comes to visit, and together they face a bully on the court.

❏ *Queen of the Court* by Michele Martin Bossley
What happens when the school's fashion queen winds up on the basketball court?

❏ *Shooting Star* by Cynthia Bates
Quyen is dealing with a troublesome teammate on her new basketball team, as well as trouble at home. Her parents seem haunted by something that happened in Vietnam.

❏ *Home Court Advantage* by Sandra Diersch
Debbie had given up hope of being adopted, until the Lowells came along. Things were looking up, until Debbie is accused of stealing from the team.

❏ *Rebound* by Adrienne Mercer
C.J.'s dream in life is to play on the national basketball team. But one day she wakes up in pain and can barely move her joints, much less be a star player.

❏ *Out of Bounds* by Gunnery Sylvia
Jay must switch schools after a house fire. He must either give up the basketball season or play alongside his rival at his new school.

❏ *Personal Best* by Gunnery Sylvia
Jay is struggling with his running skills at basketball camp but luckily for Jay, a new teammate and friend has figured out how to bring out the best in people.

Ice Hockey

❏ *The Enforcer* by Bill Swan
In this sequel to *Deflection*, Jake Henry plays goalie for his hockey

team. When the team's coach moves away, Jake's grandfather steps in to fill the role. Can the team adapt to Grandpa P.J's old-school methods?

❏ *Deflection!* by Bill Swan

Jake and his two best friends play road hockey together and are members of the same league team. But some personal rivalries and interference from Jake's three all-too-supportive grandfathers start to create tension among the players.

❏ *Misconduct* by Beverly Scudamore

Matthew has always been a popular student and hockey player. But after an altercation with a tough kid named Dillon at hockey camp, Matt finds himself number one on the bully's hit list.

❏ *Against the Boards* by Lorna Schultz Nicholson

Peter has made it onto an AAA Bantam team and is now playing hockey in Edmonton. But this shy boy from the Northwest Territories is having a hard time adjusting to his new life.

❏ *Delaying the Game* by Lorna Schultz Nicholson

When Shane comes along, Kaleigh finds herself unsure whether she can balance hockey, her friendships, and this new dating-life.

❏ *Two on One* by C.A. Forsyth

When Jeff's hockey team gets a new coach, his sister Melody starts to get more attention as the team's shining talent.

❏ *Icebreaker* by Steven Barwin

Gregg Stokes can tell you exactly when his life took a turn for the worse. It was the day his new stepsister, Amy, joined the starting line-up of his hockey team.

❏ *Too Many Men* by Lorna Schultz Nicholson

Sam has just moved with his family to Ottawa. He's quickly made first goalie on the Kanata Kings, but he feels insecure about his place on the team and at school.